"Ah, there you are." Lucas Reed walked toward her, tall and straight.

Heather's mouth went dry at the fine figure he cut in his loose linen shirt, gold waistcoat, and breeches tucked into the tops of his boots. His long, black hair was neatly tied back, emphasizing his strong jawline. No wonder Deborah fell for him. Heather straightened her spine as well as her resolve. Deborah had been a much younger woman, susceptible to the fantasies of youth, when she'd given herself to Lucas Reed, but Heather would not make the same error. Above all, she wanted a man who served God, not a blackguard who'd steal a young woman's virtue and leave her to raise their child alone.

Mr. Reed stared at her for a moment, and she couldn't help squirming. She lifted a hand to tuck a wayward strand of hair behind her ear. What did he see when he looked at her? Was he appalled by her simple garment? If not for him and his kind, she'd still be back in England, enjoying her family's wealth and the privileges that came with it. She might even be married by now and have her own child.

VICKIE McDONOUGH believes God is the ultimate designer of romance. She is a wife of thirty-four years, mother to four sons, and a doting grandma. When not writing, she enjoys reading, watching movies, and traveling. Visit Vickie's Web site at www.vickiemcdonough.com.

Books by Vickie McDonough

HEARTSONG PRESENTS
HP671—Sooner or Later
HP716—Spinning Out of Control
HP731—The Bounty Hunter and the Bride
HP747—A Wealth beyond Riches
HP816—Wild at Heart
HP831—Outlaw Heart
HP851—Straight for the Heart
HP858—A Wagonload of Trouble

Mutiny of the Heart

Vickie McDonough

Heartsong Presents

A note from the Author:
I love to hear from my readers! You may correspond with me by writing:

Vickie McDonough
Author Relations
PO Box 721
Uhrichsville, OH 44683

ISBN 978-1-61626-112-2

MUTINY OF THE HEART

All scripture quotations are taken from the King James Version of the Bible.

Our mission is to publish and distribute inspirational products offering exceptional value and biblical encouragement to the masses.

PRINTED IN THE U.S.A.

one

Charleston, South Carolina
1788

Heather Hawthorne gazed at the monstrous homes of Charleston as another wave of doubt slammed into her with the full force of a hurricane. Was she making the right decision?

Hadn't she asked herself that question a thousand times since boarding the ship back home in Canada? Was it too late to hail the carriage driver and ask him to return them to the *Charlotte Anne* before it set sail for the Caribbean?

"Are we almost there, Aunt Heather?"

Smiling down at the lad she loved as her own, she ruffled his hair then found his cap on the seat and set it on his head. "Aye, dear one, we've nearly arrived."

Jamie furrowed his brow and leaned against her arm. "Do you think he will like me?"

Heather's heart clenched as she patted his soft cheek. "Of course he will."

Please, Lord. Let it be so. Holding the lad's hand, she watched the tall homes, and even taller palm trees, pass by. She hadn't seen the likes of such houses since her family left England and settled off the coast of Canada on Nova Scotia. Her poor cottage was probably a fraction of the size of the carriage houses that sat behind many of the giant homes. Nearly all had one- and two-story porches, or piazzas as she'd heard them called. Many of them faced the Charleston harbor, welcoming the cooling breezes of the sea. She lifted her head. Though she could not see the harbor at the moment, she could smell the salty air.

Lucas Reed was said to be one of the wealthiest shipbuilders in the area and would certainly live in one of these large homes. No sooner had the thought taken wing than the coach slowed and stopped. Heather gasped and held her hand against her chest. The imposing brick house looming above them was three stories tall. The decorative front door was sheltered by a rounded portico supported by four massive white columns. Curved stairways on either side led up to the landing. Ivy clung to the brick below the portico and crept out onto the stairs, giving the home a soft accent.

The carriage driver lowered the steps and opened the door. "The home of Mr. Lucas Reed, miss."

She accepted the hand he held out and descended the steps, turning to check on Jamie. He shrank back, staring at her with wide blue eyes. "Don't be afraid, lad. I'll be with you."

He nodded then gathered the bag that held his favorite possessions and hopped down, looking around with a crinkled brow. "Where's the house?"

The driver chuckled and motioned toward the red brick structure. " 'Tis here, boy."

"But that's a big building." Jamie tilted his head back and looked up at the portico.

"Aye, the houses here are quite large."

Now that was an understatement if there ever was one. Heather swallowed the lump in her throat. She'd gone through so much to get here, but what if the man didn't want the boy?

Lucas Reed had more money than he knew what to do with from the looks of this house, and his reputation for helping others was widely talked about—although he surely hadn't helped Jamie's mother any. She pursed her lips, trying to maintain a proper attitude. She would see that he did right by the lad, even if she had to remain in this hated country to do so.

The coachman lifted out her satchel and Jamie's smaller one. "I shall run these up the stairs for you, miss."

She smiled, found a coin in her handbag, and paid the man when he returned to the coach. "Thank you for your service."

"Should I wait for you, miss?"

"Nay." Surely Mr. Reed could provide transportation back to the docks if needed. Straightening her back and her resolve, she took Jamie's hand and climbed the stairs to the massive white door. She pounded the knocker and gazed around at the homes crowded together. How could one live with neighbors so nearby?

The door opened, and she swallowed hard. A butler studied her, gazing down her length and back up. His eyes narrowed a bit. "How can I be of service?"

"We're here to see Mr. Reed. Is he at home?"

"Hmm. . .I don't remember him having an appointment today."

"We don't have one." Heather lifted her chin at the stern man. "We've just arrived in town, and I had no chance to notify Mr. Reed in advance."

Jamie tugged her hand, shuffling his feet. "I need to use the. . .you know."

The butler backed away, holding the door open. "Step inside, miss, and I'll see if Mr. Reed is available. May I tell him the nature of your business?"

" 'Tis rather private." Heather ducked her head beneath his stern gaze. She got the impression he didn't think much of her, but he wasn't the one she was worried about. They stepped inside, and he hoisted their bags and set them in the entryway then closed the door.

"Stay here. I'll return shortly. You may leave your card in the receiving tray over there." He pointed to a long, narrow table that held a hammered silver tray with three of the four corners bent inward, then strode into the interior of the house.

She wandered over to the table, taking in the fine furnishings of the home. In the dish lay several calling cards with the owners' names on them. She had no card to leave. What would it matter anyway?

"Aunt Heather. . ."

"Hang on a bit longer, please." She stooped in front of Jamie and brushed his dark hair from his deep blue eyes. Oh, how she'd miss him. He was like a son to her, but he deserved to know his father, especially since his mother had died.

But would the father be worthy of such a fine lad?

❧

Lucas Reed stood on the second-story piazza, staring at the Charleston harbor. The warm sea breeze touched his cheeks, and he lifted his head, breathing in the salty air. The morning sun glistened off the waters, causing him to squint, but even so he noticed a dolphin as it rose out of the water in a graceful arc and disappeared again.

He loved starting his mornings out here on the wide, covered porch. In fact, he just might start breaking his fast on the piazza every morning while he was in Charleston. What a perfect way to start a perfect day.

But he had business to attend to, a shipyard to oversee, and one day soon, he needed to return to the plantation and check on his servants. He donned his frock coat and took a final sip of his tea, then turned to go inside.

Langford exited the house. "There's a woman with a boy to see you, sir."

He waved his hand in dismissal. "Give them a few coins and food and send them on their way."

His butler sniffed. "Though clothed more like country folk,

I do not believe they are beggars, sir. The lady mentioned traveling and that they have just arrived this morning."

Lucas searched his mind, trying to remember what ships were due into port this week. Intrigued by the mysterious visitor, he followed Langford downstairs to the foyer. A woman of modest dress stood holding a child's hand. Her woolen gown and heavy cloak hinted that she was from a cooler climate. He wondered that she wasn't sweltering under Charleston's spring warmth.

She lifted her head and followed his downward progression with something like disdain on her pretty face. Her dark brown hair was neatly tucked under her linen cap and a wide-brimmed hat. Intelligent brown eyes stared at him without the usual signs of attraction he saw gleaming in the eyes of most women he encountered, in spite of his efforts to discourage them.

Interesting.

Women often sought him out at soirees and events, but very few actually came to his home, especially without an escort. As the elder of two sons, he'd been blessed to inherit the Reed fortune, but a not-always-unpleasant side effect was that most of the town's mamas had set their caps to snare him for their daughters. And more often than not, the town's poor found their way to his door. Somehow, he believed this woman was neither.

Langford crossed to the table where visitors left their calling cards. His mouth twitched as he picked up a tattered paper the woman must have deposited in the receiving tray. "Miss Heather Hawthorne and Master Jamie." Langford turned toward the woman. "I present Mr. Lucas Reed, miss."

Heather Hawthorne. The name meant nothing to him, and he noted that the child's last name had not been mentioned. He closed the distance between him and the woman. The boy danced at her side, tugging on her hand. Lucas resisted smiling. "Langford, perhaps you could show the boy to the facilities and then see that he has a treat in the kitchen."

Miss Hawthorne's lips tightened, and she glanced down at the child as if she didn't want to turn loose of him.

Jamie leaned toward her, shaking his legs as if cold. "Please, Aunt Heather, I must go."

Miss Hawthorne nodded, and Lucas allowed a grin, taking in the boy's black hair. When the child turned his grateful blue eyes on Lucas, his heart leaped like a horse clearing a jump. Jamie smiled, revealing a twin set of dimples, and the breath whooshed out of Lucas's lungs. His mind filled with questions, but he held his tongue until Langford and the boy were gone.

"Might I offer you a seat and some refreshment, Miss Hawthorne?"

She shook her head and fanned her face. "Nay, but I thank you."

"You have an endearing boy, Miss Hawthorne." Lucas stood with his hands locked behind his back. "May I inquire as to the nature of your business?"

The woman glanced to the doorway where Langford and the boy had quit the room; then she met his gaze. "Aye, you may. I've come to deliver your son to you."

Lucas felt as if he were riding full gallop and had encountered a tree branch hard in the chest. He opened his mouth to deny the child, but the boy's piercing blue eyes, dark hair, and dimples prevented him from speaking. He'd seen the startling resemblance of a Reed male in the boy, but he knew that he couldn't have fathered a child that age. He may have been promiscuous as a young man, but since giving his heart to God seven years ago, he hadn't been with a woman. He stared at his guest, wondering what game she was about. "I can assure you, Miss Hawthorne, that boy is not mine."

two

Heather waved her hand in front of her face as the heat of the room and the man's denial hit her full force. She took in his handsome face, black hair, and startling eyes the color of the sea. How could the arrogant rogue disallow Jamie when the boy was his miniature? Did he think she was a fortune hunter seeking to pawn off the child for the sake of a few coins? Though her heart pounded, she lifted her chin. "You are wrong, sir. Do not try to deny the lad. His face is yours."

Lucas Reed shook his head. "You are mistaken. I've never seen you before, so how could Jamie be our son? Besides, did he not call you his aunt?"

The blood rushed from her face, and she held her hand against her chest. "I never said he was mine, as much as I wish it were so. He is the son of my cousin. She is the one who assured me that Jamie was your son and made me promise to deliver him to you."

The man narrowed his eyes then waved his hand in the air. "Where is this nameless accuser? Has she not the gall to indict me to my face?"

"How dare you speak ill of the dead."

Mr. Reed's expression softened, and those startling eyes implored her to believe him, but she knew the truth. What reason could Deborah possibly have for lying about such a thing? Her cousin was amiable, genteel, and a believer in God. She would not tell a falsehood about something so important.

"I am sorry for your loss, but surely you must understand

my dilemma, miss. A stranger appears at my door with a boy she claims is mine, but I know for a fact that he couldn't be."

Her irritation surged. "You must be mistaken. 'Tis a disgrace that you could father a child and not even know about it."

His cheeks actually reddened beneath his tan. He narrowed his eyes, and she could almost see the cogs in his mind turning, trying to find a way to convince her.

"What is the name of the boy's mother?"

"Deborah Farmington."

Mr. Reed blinked, and a range of emotions flooded his handsome face. If Jamie grew up to look like his father, he'd be a comely man, for certain. And if she wasn't mistaken, the man had just gone pale. "I see you recognize Deborah's name."

His stance rigid, he turned and paced away from her, as if gathering his thoughts. His long legs carried him across the wide entryway to a room that looked like a formal parlor. The exquisite furniture must have been shipped from England, or maybe even France. Her family had owned such possessions—before her father lost his fortune funding the war against the colonists. She hated being here in this country—the country responsible for her family's demise and her father's death. Her small cottage paled in comparison, and as hard as it would be to leave the lad she loved as her own, he would have a chance to get an education here and enjoy luxuries that she could never give him.

Suddenly, Mr. Reed swerved back to face her. He strode toward her then halted and shook his head. "I'll admit to knowing Miss Farmington's name, but as I said before, it is impossible that the boy is mine."

❧

For a moment, Lucas had hoped that Jamie was his, but the years didn't add up. He hadn't seen Deborah in eight years, and the boy couldn't be more than six at the most. But even more compelling was the fact that he and Deborah had never been intimate.

Miss Hawthorne's brown eyes sparked, and she rummaged around in the worn bag that dangled from her wrist. She pulled out a crinkled paper then thrust it at him. "Here, if you don't believe me, read this."

He took the paper and turned it over, noticing the Farmington seal on the back. He rubbed his thumb over the wax, traveling back to another time. A time when he still believed in love. A time before his dreams had been crushed as effectively as a spider beneath a boot heel.

He broke the seal and began reading:

My dear Lucas,

Forgive me. I know you must be confused and most likely angry, but I implore you to accept Jamie as your own, even though you know he isn't. Surely, you can see he bears little resemblance to me, but rather has the same dark hair, remarkable blue eyes, and dimples characteristic of the Reed men. He is in fact your nephew, and Marcus's son.

Lucas sucked in a breath, drawing Miss Hawthorne's curious gaze. She obviously had no idea what message the letter held. He turned away, not wanting her to see the pain in his eyes. How could the woman he loved—the woman who was to be *his* wife—have borne a son by his brother?

His heart ached as all the memories rushed back. After a moment, he forced himself to read on:

I want you to know that I didn't go with Marcus willingly. He kidnapped me to make you suffer—to keep us from marrying. I do believe at first he saw it as a game, but then he became infatuated with me and refused to return me to you. He hates you because you inherited your father's homes and business, while he got almost nothing, even though he was born only a few minutes after you.

Lucas clutched the letter to his chest, not wanting to read what came next. Deborah hadn't left of her own accord. He'd hoped—prayed—that had been the case, and yet, as he thought back on things now, would it not have been easier on her if she had left willingly rather than as a captive aboard his brother's ship? *Oh Deborah, what you must have suffered. You have no idea how long I searched for you.*

He slowly paced the room and continued reading:

I will admit that my heart ached for Marcus after my anger died down. He seemed so lost and alone, even though I know much of it was his own doing. He took me to an island in the Caribbean where he makes his home. He said you'd know of it if you thought hard enough.

Marcus kept me two years, hoping I'd fall in love with him. Sad to say, I wish I could have. He so needed someone to love him, but my heart only ever belonged to you, Lucas.

I longed for things that must not have been God's will.

This next part is as difficult for me to write as it will be for you to hear. In a drunken rage one night, Marcus came to me and begged me to tell him I loved him. I could not.

Lucas ran his fingers through his hair, not wanting to read what followed. *Oh Deborah.*

He took me that night. I'm sorry for the crudeness of my letter, but it is vital that you understand—that no one ever know that Jamie is not your son, for consider the shame that would be cast upon him if people learn he is the illegitimate son of a pirate, the Black Mark. I'm sorry for the embarrassment and sorrows this will cause you, but for my child's sake—for the love you once held in your heart for me—I implore you to raise Jamie as your own.

I am dying. I've pleaded with my cousin Heather to bring my son to you.

I pray you walk with God and that one day I will see you in heaven.

I shall remain forever yours,
Deborah

Lucas leaned against the doorjamb, trying to grasp all the letter had said. He clenched his fist, knowing if he ever saw his brother again, he'd flog him within an inch of his life. He sighed and forced his hand to relax.

He'd loved his brother, but they had never been close, even though they were twins. Their father had showed his favoritism toward Lucas from the time they were small. He knew it, and Marcus knew it. As a young boy, Marcus had been content with his mother's attention—but not as he grew older and the reality of his situation sank in. He'd become increasingly disgruntled, and his behavior was abysmal.

Keeping the child could well damage Lucas's fine reputation. He considered Jamie, and his heart took wing. Could the boy be a gift from God? Lucas was being given the chance to raise Deborah's son—the boy that should have been *his* son. Keeping Jamie would change many things in Lucas's life. And what did he know about raising a child? Nothing. Yet he couldn't turn family away. Jamie was Deborah's son—and from this day forward, Jamie would become his son. He smacked the letter against his fist, his decision made, and turned to face the woman. "The boy can stay."

Relief washed over her face a moment before she buried her cheeks in her hands.

"Is that not what you want?" Lucas asked.

"Aye. But how will I ever say good-bye to him? He's such a young lad. I've tended him ever since his mother died three years ago."

Lucas jerked back as if he'd been struck. "Three years! Why did you wait so long to bring him here?"

Miss Hawthorne's cheeks matched the red of his parlor settee, and she ducked her head. "I do not have the means you do. It took me this long to raise the money for the trip, and had I not traveled with a friend of my father's, I'd not be here now."

"Why did you not write me? I could have sent the funds for passage."

She looked at him with skepticism. "I did not know how you'd receive the news and thought it better to come in person so that you could see how much Jamie resembles you."

Lucas narrowed his eyes. "And how is it you knew that when we've never met before?"

"Deborah said Jamie was the spitting image of his father."

"Indeed." Fortunately, he and his brother were identical twins. No one need ever know that Jamie wasn't his son, no matter the scourge Lucas may face among his friends and business associates for birthing an illegitimate child. For the boy's sake, he'd endure whatever came his way.

At the sound of footsteps, he turned. Jamie trotted toward him, his relief evident when he saw Miss Hawthorne. Lucas glanced at her, noting again her simple beauty. Leaving Jamie would be terribly difficult for her, he was certain. He rubbed his chin with his thumb and forefinger. And what of the boy? He'd already lost his mother. The separation from his guardian could be devastating. Lucas would need a governess to care for the boy. Turning, he watched as Miss Hawthorne bent and gave Jamie a hug. Perhaps it would work best if she'd be willing to stay on until he could hire someone permanently. That would allow Jamie time to become comfortable in his new home and with him before Miss Hawthorne left.

"Miss Abigail gave me corn pudding and a sweet roll." Jamie's eyes glowed.

"You'll have no room for your supper now," Miss Hawthorne teased. She smoothed the hair out of Jamie's eyes.

Lucas's heart swelled with love for the boy he'd just met. How was that possible? He shook his head and turned to his servant. "Langford, see that the room next to mine is made ready for Master Jamie."

Langford was a British immigrant who rarely showed emotion or expression of any kind, but at Lucas's order, the butler's gray eyes went wide. He looked from the woman to the child and back then leaned forward. "Surely you do not mean to keep the urchin, sir."

Lucas lifted a brow, surprised that Langford would question him, especially in public. "Please do as I say. As you can well see, the boy has my blood. He is a Reed and, as such, will be living here and deserves the same respect you'd give me. Is that clear?"

Langford's lips twitched, and his eyes narrowed, as if he thought Lucas had been taken in by a pretty wench and a sad story. But he dipped his head and started up the stairs.

Jamie tugged on Miss Hawthorne's skirt. "Are you staying, too?"

She blinked her eyes and bent down, allowing Jamie to hug her neck. Patting his back, she said, "Shh. . .child, you belong with your father now."

"I don't have a father," Jamie wailed. "I want to stay with you."

"Aye, you do, and he's standing right there, waiting to get to know you."

Sniffing, Jamie turned his head but kept it resting on Miss Hawthorne's shoulder as he eyed Lucas. He offered the boy a smile and now regretted his initial harshness. But there were many who'd take advantage of his wealth, and while he didn't mind helping the poor, he wouldn't be taken in by a miscreant bent on swindling him.

Stooping down, he hoped to make himself less intimidating. "How would you like it if Miss Hawthorne were to stay awhile, too?"

A light sparked in Jamie's eyes, making Lucas want to please the boy. Jamie leaned back and gazed up at her face. "Would you, Aunt Heather? Stay here with me?"

She stood and straightened her dress then lifted a brow to Lucas.

He realized he should have asked her before getting Jamie's hopes up. "Could you stay a fortnight or so, to allow me time to find a proper governess and to give Jamie time to get to know me before you take your leave?"

Her gaze roved the house, and he wondered what she saw. She seemed uncomfortable in his home. Had she never before lived in such a setting? He tried to see the home from her eyes, but everything was so familiar that he couldn't. Once again, he realized how much God had entrusted to him, and he determined to do what he could to help others.

Miss Hawthorne glanced down at her clothing. "I would like to stay and see Jamie settled, but I don't belong here. I would embarrass you with my clothing and my lack of knowledge of American life. And I must catch the *Charlotte Anne* on her way back from the Caribbean to return home."

"Nonsense. Everyone in my employment receives the proper clothing and instruction for their position, although,

I suppose you know far more about tending the boy than anyone here. I'll see to it that you have some new clothes, and perhaps you could help me interview governesses. When the time comes for you to return, I'll find a place for you on one of my ships."

"Say aye, Aunt Heather." Jamie smiled and peered up at Miss Hawthorne. "We can *both* stay."

The woman gazed up at Lucas, and he had a difficult time not fidgeting. She stared at him as if taking his measure, but finally she nodded. "Aye, we'll both stay, for the time being."

Lucas smiled, grateful the woman was willing to remain for a time for the boy's sake. Langford made his way down the stairs and stopped in front of him. "The room is being readied, sir."

"Thank you. Now, I need you to inform the upstairs maid to make ready a room near the boy's for Miss Hawthorne. She'll be staying to care for Jamie until I hire a governess."

Langford's nostrils flared, but he dipped his head. "As you wish, sir." As he retrieved their bags and turned toward the stairs again, Lucas was certain he heard the man mutter, "Highly irregular."

He resisted smiling again and shook his head. Today he'd become the father of his brother's son. Yes sir. Highly irregular.

three

"I'm starving, Aunt Heather." Jamie rubbed his stomach. "Something downstairs sure smells good."

"Aye, and we'd better get down there, or we'll not get to eat." She took her ward's hand and escorted him down the grand staircase. Last night she'd slept in a bed as big as her whole sleeping chamber back home, and it had been so soft she'd felt as if she were resting on a cloud.

"This house is bigger than any in Nova Scotia." Jamie stared wide-eyed up at the fancy ceiling with its decorative plaster works.

"I don't know as it's bigger, but it certainly is fancier."

She stepped onto the entryway floor as Jamie leaned toward her. "Mr. Reed sure must be rich. You think he'd buy me a pony?"

"Oh Jamie. You disappoint me." Heather shook her head and stared down at him. "You should be happy that you've been united with your father and not worry about things of the world."

Jamie ducked his head and kicked the bottom step with his shoe. "Aye, mum."

She tugged him close. How could she begrudge him wanting something nice? He'd had precious few things to call his own his whole life. Heather walked toward the kitchen, unsure where they would be expected to eat. She shook her head at the opulence around her. Yet as she studied the home, she realized the furniture was expensive but functional, and there seemed to be few useless extravagances and more practical items.

Her family had enjoyed wealth—not to the extreme the

Reeds did, but enough that they had lived a comfortable life. At least until the colonists rose up to fight for their independence. Her father had sunk his fortune into the war efforts, but in the end, Britain lost, and the Hawthorne family had little left. Her father, born into a wealthy family, was unacquainted with poverty and all but lost his will to live, finally succumbing a year ago. For that, she'd always despise the colonists—Americans, as they now called themselves.

"Ah, there you are." Lucas Reed walked toward her, tall and straight.

Heather's mouth went dry at the fine figure he cut in his loose linen shirt, gold waistcoat, and breeches tucked into the tops of his boots. His long, black hair was neatly tied back, emphasizing his strong jawline. No wonder Deborah fell for him. Heather straightened her spine as well as her resolve. Deborah had been a much younger woman, susceptible to the fantasies of youth, when she'd given herself to Lucas Reed, but Heather would not make the same error. Above all, she wanted a man who served God, not a blackguard who'd steal a young woman's virtue and leave her to raise their child alone.

Mr. Reed stared at her for a moment, and she couldn't help squirming. She lifted a hand to tuck a wayward strand of hair behind her ear. What did he see when he looked at her? Was he appalled by her simple garment? If not for him and his kind, she'd still be back in England, enjoying her family's wealth and the privileges that came with it. She might even be married by now and have her own child.

"You must find those wool dresses dreadfully uncomfortable in the heat of the South. We need to make our first stop the dressmakers."

Heather's cheeks felt as if she'd brushed up against the flame of a candle. How dare he. "I don't believe my clothing is a proper topic of conversation."

The rogue had the gall to chuckle. "We can't have you fainting dead away from the heat, can we?"

Jamie tugged on Mr. Reed's waistcoat. "I'm hungry, sir."

Lucas squatted down. "Are you now? We should do something about that then. Come."

He took Jamie's hand, and the boy followed along, already trusting the man. Heather's heart cracked. All too soon, Jamie would become comfortable here, and she'd have to leave, never to see him again. How could she bear it?

At the doorway, Jamie looked back over his shoulder. "Come on, Aunt Heather."

She smiled, her fears tempered for the moment. Mr. Reed surprised her by sitting Jamie at the large table in the dining room. Most wealthy people relegated their young children to eating in the kitchen or the nursery. "Wouldn't you rather Jamie and I ate in the kitchen?"

"Bah! I don't cotton to family not taking meals together. I'm sure Jamie will behave himself. Won't you, boy?"

Jamie nodded then reached for a sweet roll. Heather shook her head, and the lad's eyes widened, but he lowered his hand to his lap. She sat, waiting for Mr. Reed to begin dining, but he just looked at her with those piercing eyes.

"Before meals, I like to thank the good Lord for my food. Do you mind?" he said.

She shook her head, even though she felt uncomfortable. Her father had never believed in God and had refused to allow prayers at mealtime.

"Can you bow your head, Jamie?"

"Aye, sir." Jamie ducked his head, but he peered up at Heather.

"Close your eyes, son." Lucas smiled.

Son. Family. Heather's heartbeat raced at the words. Why would Lucas Reed so easily accept the child he'd adamantly denied yesterday? Until she'd given him Deborah's letter, he'd been less than convinced. She glanced down at her hands while Mr. Reed blessed the food.

When she returned home, she'd be all alone. Jamie had helped her heart, still aching from her father's death, heal with his easy smile and frequent hugs. Oh how she'd miss him. Her eyes misted, but she blinked them dry and reached for the platter of sliced ham that Mr. Reed held out to her.

"So, Jamie, tell me what you like to do." Mr. Reed spooned porridge into his bowl and then added some honey.

Jamie sat on his knees and reached for the sweet roll again. Heather decided to try a flaky bread shaped like a half-moon.

"Aunt Heather's teaching me my letters and how to read some."

Lucas nodded and smiled. " 'Tis a good thing for a boy to know how to read at such a young age."

Jamie sat a bit straighter. Lucas dished up a smaller bowl of porridge and passed it to him. "What else do you do?"

Jamie's eyes lifted toward the ceiling as he contemplated the question. "I help Aunt Heather make soap."

One of Mr. Reed's brows quirked up. "Indeed."

Heather nodded, wondering what he thought of her profession. She needed some way to provide for herself and Jamie.

"Aye. Indeed," Jamie parroted. "I gather the wood for the fire."

As the meal progressed, Heather relaxed. In spite of the ire she held toward Lucas Reed for what he'd done to Deborah, she found the man likable and comfortable to be around. He didn't maintain the snobbish reserve she'd expected from someone of his stature in society and wealth.

When they were nearly finished with their meal, Langford strode in, his nose lifted high as if he were the one with all the money. "Waverly is here from the stable, sir."

"Very good." Lucas turned his gaze on Jamie. "How would you like to visit the stable and see my horses?"

Jamie bounced back up on his knees. "Truly? Aye, I would." His gaze faltered as it shifted toward Heather. "Is it all right if I go?"

She nodded. "Aye, but you should now be asking such questions of your father when he is in the room."

"But he's the one who asked *me*."

Lucas chuckled. "I did at that."

"Will you go, too?" Jamie asked her.

"I'd like to have a talk with Miss Hawthorne," Mr. Reed interjected, "if you are agreeable."

Jamie eyed them both then shrugged. "All right." Then he grinned. "I get to see the horses while you two just get to talk."

Lucas smiled, but the look he gave Heather sent a warm shiver down her back and made her think he felt he was getting the better end of the bargain. If she didn't keep her guard up, she'd quickly be disarmed by his charm and friendliness.

"Go with Langford, and then Mr. Waverly will escort you to the stable. Be sure that you do as Waverly says, and don't get overly close to the horses. We'll be right here in this room until you return."

"Promise?"

"Jamie, you heard the man. Do not question your father." Heather knew he was afraid she'd leave while he was gone. How would he bear their permanent separation?

"Aye, mum."

Mr. Reed watched with pride in his eyes as Jamie followed Langford out of the room; then he switched his unnerving gaze on her. "Would you care for more tea, Miss Hawthorne?"

Startled by his offer to serve her, she simply shook her head. Finally, she found her voice and pointed to the pastry she'd eaten. "These are quite good and so light."

"I fancy them myself. I first had one on a trip to France."

"They're delicious."

Mr. Reed nodded. "Jamie is a fine boy. You've done well with him, especially since he wasn't your own child."

Her heart clenched. Though he had complimented her, he'd only reinforced that the lad wasn't hers to keep.

"Thank you for bringing him here. I only wish I'd known about him before now." He stared into his cup, and she thought he truly meant what he'd said.

"So, how did Deborah come to live with you?"

Heather's ire returned, shoving away any compassion she might have felt for the man. "She was with child, unmarried, and too ashamed to return to her parents' home."

Mr. Reed had the good sense to wince at her intentional barb. "Yes, well, if only she had come to me, I'd have done right by her."

She wanted to ask how he could be intimate with a woman of Deborah's quality and then turn her aside like a trollop, but she couldn't voice the words. How could he dally with a woman's affections, take what he wanted, and just cast her away like bilge water? What she knew about Lucas Reed didn't match the kind, open man before her. It was as if they were two different people.

"Tell me about the Hawthornes. You have an English surname, but your Christian name is Scottish, I believe. Have you always lived in Canada?"

"Nay, not always. My mother's heritage is Scottish, but my father's is English. About four years ago, shortly after my mother died, my father and I left England and settled in Nova Scotia. He is also dead now." She left off the cause of her father's death. Though she blamed the colonists and their desire for independence from England for her family's demise, it was hardly fair to hold Mr. Reed personally to blame.

He studied her for a moment, as if deciphering the reason for her angst. He sipped his tea then set down the cup. "My family was originally from England, too, although my grandfather moved to Barbados before coming to the colonies. I've visited relatives in England and done business there but have always called America my home. Besides this house, I own a plantation called Reed Springs. I'd like to take you and Jamie there sometime soon, after I conclude my business here. I think he'd be more comfortable where he has land for running around. And before you worry about us traveling together without a chaperone, my neighbors the Madisons will journey with us. They traveled here with me a fortnight ago, and we're to return together. Also, my mother resides at the plantation."

Heather nodded. She should be amazed that the man owned another home besides this one, but she wasn't. She'd heard that many people who lived in Charleston had second homes they went to in order to get away from the summer heat and the annoying mosquitoes and gnats that invaded the coastal regions. Suddenly, she realized he'd mentioned his mother. Heather had never considered that Jamie might have grandparents still living. How would Mrs. Reed react to Jamie? Would she embrace him as her grandson or find him a family embarrassment?

Mr. Reed steepled his fingertips. "How did Deborah die, if I may ask?"

"From an extended illness. Jamie's birth was hard on her, and she never quite regained her health." Died of a broken heart was more like it.

"I'm sorry. I wish I could have helped her."

He hung his head, and she truly believed he meant what

he said. Perhaps over the years, the man had changed from the scoundrel who'd stolen Deborah's innocence. But she didn't want to feel compassion for him. She stared out a nearby window at a line of shrubs covered in brilliant pink flowers. That was something she'd noticed right off on arriving in South Carolina—the abundance of beautiful flowers. And the moss that swung from the trees like lace drying on limbs gave the place a homey feel. So different from Canada, which had barely begun to thaw.

Mr. Reed tapped his finger on the table. "What do you suppose I should look for in a governess?"

His rapid topic changes continued to take her by surprise. She dreaded some other woman taking care of Jamie, but there was no helping it. "Someone who is kind and loves children, I suppose. Someone who is patient and will be a good instructor."

"That sounds like you."

"Thank you, sir." She turned her head away as her cheeks warmed. She would have to keep her defenses raised to avoid being charmed by this rogue, and keeping Deborah in mind did just the trick. She would have to watch herself so that she, too, wasn't taken in by the beguiling Lucas Reed.

"The Madisons will arrive at ten. I thought you'd feel more comfortable having another woman along as we shop for your clothing."

"We?" She lifted a brow to him. "Do you normally purchase your servants' clothing yourself?"

He grinned wide. "No, but Jamie needs apparel better suited to our warmer climate, too, and I thought we'd go together. There are times I'll be busy with work and may not see Jamie for a while, so I'd like to spend this day getting to know him."

She nodded. "We shall be ready by ten."

four

Heather liked Caroline Madison immediately. At Mr. Reed's introduction, the lively blond flitted away from her tall, dashing husband and came to stand before her. There were obvious questions in the woman's gaze, but she was polite enough not to voice them.

Mr. Reed introduced them all, lightly touching Jamie's shoulder when he gave the lad's name: Jamie Reed. At last, Deborah's son wore the surname that truly belonged to him.

"Welcome, to Charleston, Miss Hawthorne. It's a pleasure to meet you."

Heather nodded. "And you, too."

Mrs. Madison bent toward Jamie and ruffled his hair. "And aren't you just the spitting image of your father?"

Jamie's gaze darted to his father, as if he'd never considered they might resemble each other. Mr. Reed's bright smile and sparkling eyes led her to believe he was proud of Jamie. Certainly not the reaction she'd expected from a wealthy man whose illegitimate son had suddenly invaded his life. Evidently he'd informed the Madisons of the situation before she and Jamie had come back downstairs. How had he gone about explaining the presence of a five-year-old son he'd never laid eyes on before?

"Shall we be off?" Mr. Reed reached for a tricorne hat that hung on the hall tree in the entryway and set it on his head.

"Are we to ride in a carriage, sir?"

Mr. Reed smiled down at Jamie. "No son, it's a lovely day and not far, so we shall walk."

The men took the lead with the women and Jamie

following. Nearly six feet tall, Mr. Madison stood only a few inches shorter than Mr. Reed. They seemed good friends and carried on a lively conversation.

"I do have to say Lucas certainly surprised Richard and me upon our arrival when he shared his exciting news with us." Mrs. Madison glanced down at Jamie. "Besides my husband, Lucas is the most honorable man I know. I cannot believe he'd"—she leaned close to Heather's ear—"father a child and not marry the mother and raise the boy."

Heather clenched her hands together, not caring to talk about the subject. If Mrs. Madison wanted information, she'd need to direct her questions to Mr. Reed. "Have you always lived in Charleston?"

"No, I was born in Boston. My family moved here when I was only twelve. Father wanted to get away from the cold weather, and we've lived here ever since. We do, however, visit our Boston relatives during the heat of the summer. Richard's family is from here, though. He's the third generation of Madisons born in this area."

They walked several short blocks then crossed a wide street to where a number of vendors were selling their wares. All manner of food was sold in booths and shops. Jamie tugged on her skirt, and Heather looked down.

"What's she doing?" He pointed at a dark-skinned woman weaving a basket that looked to be made of straw.

"Those are sweetgrass baskets," Mrs. Madison said. "They're made from marsh grasses that are harvested along the coast."

"That's fascinating. So they braid the grasses into platters and containers?" Heather asked.

"Not braid. If you look at the unbound grass, you can see that they are just long stems that are secured together with a strip of palm leaf wrapped around them."

"The tradition of making the sweetgrass trays and baskets

was brought over by slaves from Africa," Mr. Reed added.

Jamie leaned against her skirt. "Is that woman a slave?"

Heather patted his shoulder. "I don't know."

"She probably is, as are the other weavers here." Mr. Reed gazed down the street and shook his head. "I know most planters rely on slave labor, but I think owning another man is atrocious."

Heather stared at the man, surprised that he'd so openly voiced his disgust of slavery, which was a common institution in the South. She'd heard there had been slaves ever since the first ship arrived here. How did Mr. Reed run his plantation without the aid of slaves? Didn't he mention growing rice? Producing such a crop surely took numerous servants.

"You see those big platters made from grass, Jamie?" Mr. Madison said. "Those are called *fannahs*. The field-workers place rice in them then toss the rice up into the air and catch it again in the fannah. The air blows away the chaff—the bad parts—and leaves the hull."

"Oh." Jamie studied the trays with woven handles on each end as if trying to visualize the process.

Mr. Reed patted Jamie's head. "You'll get to see it done when we go to the plantation."

"Can I try it?"

Mr. Reed grinned. "That's a splendid idea. You'll need to learn every aspect of plantation work if you're going to run Reed Springs one day."

"Truly?" Jamie's eyes widened as he stared up at his father.

Heather's heart jolted. Surely the man wasn't thinking in such a direction already. Why, he'd only met Jamie yesterday. She didn't want him falsely raising the lad's hopes. Someday Lucas Reed would marry. In fact, she was surprised that he didn't already have a wife, and that wife—once he did acquire one—would expect *her* son to inherit the Reed properties, not her husband's illegitimate child.

"Well, I hope for my sake that isn't anytime soon." Mr. Reed chuckled. "Are you ready to go see a couple of my ships, son?"

"Aye, sir. I am."

"Might I broach a suggestion?" Mrs. Madison stepped forward. "We care as little for the roughness of the dock area as I'm sure you do for a dressmaker's shop. Why don't you menfolk visit the docks while I take Miss Hawthorne to purchase what she needs? Then we can meet up and see to Jamie's clothing."

Mr. Reed's gaze collided with Heather's, and her pulse shot forward like a startled horse. "Would that be agreeable with you?" he asked.

She nodded. "Aye. There is no sense in you men having to wait around for us." Not to mention she'd be terribly embarrassed to purchase clothing with them watching.

"So you don't mind if Jamie goes along with us?"

Her heart somersaulted at the thought of parting with the boy. "I'd thought to take him with us," she said.

"But I want to see the ships." Jamie's pleading gaze bored into hers.

She almost shook her head. Only a day ago, he'd been anxious to get off the ship that brought them to Charleston, and now he longed to see one again. Fickle boy. The truth be told, it was too soon for *her* to be separated from him. Yet he needed to gradually get used to the idea, and she needed to know she could trust Lucas Reed with Jamie's well-being. This was a perfect opportunity for a short parting. "Aye, 'tis fine with me if you go with your father, but be sure that you obey him."

"I will." Jamie bounced on his toes and clapped his hands, making his father smile.

Mr. Reed reached down and took Jamie's hand. "Shall we meet up at McCrady's at noon?"

Mrs. Madison nodded. "Noon should be perfect."

Mr. Reed grinned, warming Heather's insides. He looked down at Jamie. "Shall we be off then?"

She watched the men cross the street, and on the other side, Lucas Reed stooped down and said something to Jamie. The lad nodded, and his father hoisted him up into his arms. Jamie looped one arm around Mr. Reed's neck then turned back and grinned at Heather and waved.

"They're getting along famously, aren't they?"

"Aye." Almost too well. As much as she wanted Jamie and his father to have a good relationship, Heather dreaded seeing him distance himself from her, but it had to be. Once Mr. Reed hired another governess, she'd be on her way back to Canada.

"And it's kind of Lucas to be so concerned with your feelings."

Heather glanced sideways at the woman. "What do you mean?"

Mrs. Madison giggled and waved her hand in the air. "Nothing actually. It's just that most men in Lucas's situation wouldn't ask if it was all right with the governess to take his own son somewhere."

Heather winced. Though the words were spoken casually, she felt rightly put in her place. She may have been the one to raise Jamie and bring him here, but she was just the hired help now. Then why had Mrs. Madison taken it upon herself to escort her to the dressmaker's shop instead of letting Mr. Reed's housekeeper do that?

Two hours later, Heather's legs ached. She had stood still while the dressmaker measured her, had tried on several ready-made items that the woman had in stock, as well as stood in front of a mirror while the other two women decided which colors looked best on her. The result was two fancy silk gowns for evening wear, one green with a gold-striped petticoat and the other a lovely lavender with soft blue accents. The three day dresses made of lightweight linen would feel much more comfortable in the heat of the afternoon, but what excited Heather the most was the new drawers, chemise, stockings, and petticoats. She hadn't had any new undergarments other than those she'd sewn herself from rough fabrics since she left England. If only she didn't have to wait until the dressmaker made them. At least she'd be able to wear the one ready-made day dress that was to be delivered to Mr. Reed's house later this afternoon.

"I especially liked how you looked in that dark green gown. It goes well with your coloring." Mrs. Madison waved her lovely silk fan in front of her face. "You will love the linen fabric. It's less formal but necessary here and much cooler than wool."

Heather struggled to keep up with the taller woman's longer stride. "I think you purchased far too many outfits. I could have easily made do with less."

"Fiddlesticks. If you hadn't been so persuasive, I'd have ordered more garments. Lucas said to be sure you had all you needed."

"I'm only going to be here until he hires another governess. Perhaps if he employs someone close to me in size, she will be able to use the same clothing. I've little need of lightweight dresses in Canada."

"Who knows?" The woman waved her hand in the air and dashed across the street. Then slowing her steps, she peered over her shoulder. "Perhaps you will be here longer than you think."

Heather hurried, not wanting to be left behind. She fell in behind Mrs. Madison to allow a man and his wife to pass, then hurried back to her side. "Why do you say that?"

Mrs. Madison shrugged. "Just a hunch, my dear. You're the best person to raise Jamie. You've been with him all his life, is that not correct?"

Heather nodded. "Aye, 'tis true."

"Well, then how could another woman be better than you?"

Heather's heart soared then plummeted like a quail spooked from the grass and shot from the sky. She'd love to be there for Jamie, but how could she stay in this country she so despised? Her family had lost everything because of the colonists' bid for freedom.

She contemplated the woman's words as they continued down the street past a silver shop where fine quality cups, platters, and jewelry were displayed in a window. The hammer of a cobbler reached her ears as they walked past his open door. A young boy stood in front of a printer's shop, hawking papers. Charleston certainly was a busy place.

Could she live in this country and put aside her feelings for Jamie's sake? She'd never considered that could be an option and wasn't sure now that it was, but so far the people she'd met had been more than kind and receiving, not the rebellious troublemakers she'd half expected to encounter.

"Ah, there's McCrady's now. I hope the men are already there. I'm famished."

One thing was for certain, Heather would have to think long and hard before making a decision to stay in America—if Lucas Reed even asked her to.

❧

Lucas couldn't remember a more enjoyable morning. Jamie had tossed questions at him faster than a clipper could speed across the ocean at full sail. The boy was smart, curious, and well behaved.

"How many ships can you build in a year?" Jamie asked.

"Well now, that depends on any number of things. The

weather for one. Also, the availability of skilled workmen."

"Perhaps I'll be a shipbuilder when I grow up."

Lucas caught Richard's amused glance and smiled.

"Maybe you will, son." He ruffled Jamie's hair then recaptured his hand. The child seemed to trust him totally and had expressed no fear being away from Miss Hawthorne, even though well over an hour had passed.

"I have to say, I don't believe I've seen you looking happier, Lucas, than you have today." Richard nodded.

"I am happy." Warmth flooded Lucas's chest. With Jamie's arrival, he realized how lonely he'd been. How much he'd wanted a family but had been afraid of pursuing a woman. What if his brother found out about her and decided to purloin her as he had Deborah? He clenched his fist. Marcus would have to get past him first.

"I hope you realize what a blessing from God the boy is."

Lucas relaxed his fist. "I surely do. I can't help thinking over and over how much he will change my life."

Richard cleared his throat and leaned a bit closer as they strode down the street. "I don't suppose I need to tell you that there are likely to be repercussions. While I, for one, think it's an honorable thing you've done, some people will look down on you for taking in the boy or for not marrying his mother when you learned she was with child."

Skirting a pile of manure in the street, Lucas cast his friend a quick glance. "I never knew about him until he and Miss Hawthorne arrived at my door."

"Well, it's hard to believe you didn't expect the possibility of a child when. . ." Richard waved his hand in the air. "You know."

Lucas clapped his hand on his friend's shoulder. "You're my closest friend, Richard, but there are things even you don't know. I'm asking you to trust me on this, and I hope I have your support whatever the result may be."

"Of course you have it, and don't feel you have to explain things to me. What man doesn't harbor a few secrets?"

"Thank you. I appreciate your friendship. Even though I've only known you a few years, I feel closer to you than many people I've known all my life."

Richard swatted a fly away from his face. "When a man becomes a believer in Christ, he becomes part of the family of God. We're more than friends; we're brothers."

Lucas smiled. It was true. He thought of his friends who were Christians and knew that he was close to them in a way he wasn't with unbelievers. Now that he was a father, he'd need to teach Jamie about the Lord. He'd better read up on what the Bible had to say about children. A verse from Proverbs popped into his mind: *"Correct thy son, and he shall give thee rest; yea, he shall give delight unto thy soul."*

His father had certainly taken pleasure in quoting verses on disciplining children, although it hadn't helped Marcus. Lucas had come to resent the quotes, too, because they often occurred before a punishment. Could that, perchance, be the reason he hadn't become a believer in God until well into his manhood?

"Fresh fish fer sale. Oysters, lobsters, and the like."

Jamie stopped and watched the near-toothless hawker. "He looks like Mr. Simons from back home."

"Does he now?" Lucas patted his son's head. How long would it take before Jamie called Charleston home?

"Aye, but Mr. Simons has teeth. Big ones."

Lucas chuckled at how Jamie widened his eyes when he'd said *big*. "And what type of work did that man do?"

Jamie shrugged. "Don't know. He just came around a lot, wanting to talk to Aunt Heather." His brow crinkled. "I don't think she liked it when he visited."

Had this Mr. Simons been a suitor? Or perhaps he'd had more nefarious ideas. Lucas hated the thought of Miss Hawthorne alone and having that man pay a visit. Why did the man not bring a chaperone if he had noble plans?

"I'm hungry. Are we about there?" Jamie rubbed his stomach.

"Yes son, it's not much farther." Maybe he should have hired a coach, but the day was fair and he'd thought the walk would be good for them all. He slowed his pace so that Jamie didn't have to work so hard to keep up.

Charleston was bustling this morning with women out shopping before the heat of the afternoon arrived. Businessmen stood chatting, while slaves and common workers hauled various items in wagons and handcarts. Lucas loved this town and hoped his son would come to feel the same way.

"Well now, 're ye not a sight for sore eyes?"

Off to his right, a woman dressed in near rags pushed away from the door of a tavern. He looked around but saw no one other than himself and Richard close enough for her to be addressing. She took three quick steps and leapt in front of him so that he had to stop or knock her down. Jamie peered up at her then pinched his nose to ward off her foul odor.

"Don'tcha remember me?" She reached out and felt the edge of Lucas's frock coat with her grimy fingers. "Ye clean up quite good, ye do. 'Re ye pretending to be a gentleman?"

Richard slowed and turned, lifting his brows as if to ask, *Who's that?*

Lucas shrugged and motioned to Jamie. "Go with Richard, son, and I'll meet the two of you at McCrady's shortly. Your aunt Heather may have already arrived." He handed the boy off to Richard. "See that you obey Mr. Madison."

"Aye, sir." Jamie watched over his shoulder with a worried expression as Richard led him down the street. For a child who'd not had a father until now and had lost his mother at such a young age, he was quite well behaved and compliant.

"What's the matter, dearie? Ye forget me purty face already?"

Lucas refocused on the trollop. "I've never before laid eyes on you, madam."

She swatted her hand in the air. "It's Lilly. Ye cain't forget what a fine time we had aboard yer ship, can ye?"

Lucas bristled. Until now, he'd thought she was just a beggar out to earn a coin, but she must be confusing him with his brother. When had Marcus been in Charleston? A shiver charged down his spine. He couldn't let his brother learn about Jamie.

"I fear you are mistaking me for someone else, madam."

The woman cackled, revealing yellowed teeth with a good number missing. Though filthy, she hardly looked old enough to be losing her teeth. Perhaps a few had been knocked out by less accommodating men.

"Ye cain't fool me." She leaned in closer, bringing her wretched scent along. "Ye're the Black Mark, ain'tcha?"

Lucas straightened and glanced around to see if anyone had heard the woman. "I am not. But can you tell me how long ago he was here? Is he returning?"

Her hazel eyes narrowed. "Hmm. . .I don't reckon ye're him, after all. Ye have the look and speech of a real gentleman." Her gaze softened, and she leaned against his arm. He stepped back, causing her to stumble, and he reached out to steady her.

"If ye ain't Marcus Reed, then ye must be his twin brother."

Lucas blinked, surprised at her comment. Did she mean that factually, or was she just making a random comment that he closely resembled Marcus? "Does the man you talk of have a twin?"

"He has a brother—or so says the Black Mark—but I know not if he be a twin." She peered over her shoulder to the spot where he'd last seen Jamie before he went around the corner. "But he never mentioned that brother having a son that looks just like 'im."

A fear he'd never before encountered enveloped Lucas. What if his brother learned about Jamie? Would the boy ever be safe?

He reached into his pocket and pulled out two gold coins. The woman's eyes sparked as her hand slithered out. He lifted the coins above her head. "For your silence, madam."

Her gaze narrowed but lifted toward the coins. She licked her lips and nodded. Lucas dropped the bribe into her filthy hand then hurried toward McCrady's. Paying a bribe was wrong. He knew that. But he could not let his unscrupulous brother get his hands on an innocent child.

five

Heather watched the last vestige of Charleston disappear as the ship glided around a bend in the Ashley River. She was silly to fear venturing into the unknown again, but she couldn't shake her nervousness. Just as it had happened on the *Charlotte Anne*, civilization fell away, and she entered an unfamiliar world. She tightened her grip on Jamie's hand.

"Ow, that hurts." He tugged his hand away and stood on tiptoes to see over the ship's gunwale.

Behind them, Mr. Reed barked orders to his men. She rubbed Jamie's hair, her heart aching. This journey inland was the beginning of the end of their time together. On her return trip, she'd be alone—truly alone for the first time in her life. How could such a wee lad have been her lifeline?

"Look at that bird!" Jamie swatted her skirt with one hand and pointed toward the shoreline with his other.

Caroline Madison left her husband's side near the middle of the ship and sashayed toward them. "That's a heron. One of the larger species."

As if annoyed at them for invading his territory, the bird turned toward the ship, opened its long beak, and screeched out a call that sounded somewhere between a croak and a hack. Jamie giggled and attempted to shinny up the topsides and onto the gunwale to get a closer look. Heather grabbed him before he toppled over and into the water and hauled him back down.

"We have birds like that in Nova Scotia," he said.

"It may be from Canada. Some birds migrate down here," Caroline said. "There are many interesting creatures in the marshlands. Just mind that you don't go near the river's edge. Alligators inhabit the waters around here."

Heather's gaze snapped to Caroline's. "Are there any at Reed Springs?"

"I don't recall ever seeing one there, but take caution if you go near any of the ponds or the river."

The two men joined them. "Yes," Mr. Reed said, "we have alligators. 'Tis my greatest concern for the workers in my rice fields. That and snakes."

Heather's hand lifted to her neck. Snakes and alligators. What kind of place was Mr. Reed taking his son to?

He glanced at her and smiled.

Her stomach lurched.

"Have no fear, Miss Hawthorne. Jamie will be quite safe. It may sound as if we live in the wilderness, but I believe you will be pleasantly surprised at the quality of our plantation home."

"Yes, Reed Springs is a fine, sturdy place." Mrs. Madison said. "Amazingly, it survived our fight for independence when many of our fine homes did not. The British burned so many of them. What a dreadful shame."

Heather winced but tried to ignore the comment. Caroline did not know her past.

Jamie tugged on the bottom of Mr. Reed's frock coat. Heather reached for the boy, but his father hoisted him up in his arms. "What is it, son?"

"This ship is smaller than your other ones. Why didn't we take one of the big ones?"

"Ah, an excellent question." Mr. Reed waved his free hand toward the middle of the vessel. "This is a cutter, and the reason we're taking it is because the river is fairly shallow and the draft of a cutter is less than a ship."

"What's a draft?" Jamie stared at the man with blank eyes.

" 'Tis the vertical length of the keel."

Jamie blinked. "What's a keel?"

Mr. Madison chuckled. "You're going to have to teach the boy all about sailing vessels, Lucas."

"That is something to which I look forward." Mr. Reed smiled. "And there's no better time than the present." He turned with Jamie in his arms and walked toward the center of the cutter. "A cutter is a fore-and-aft rigged vessel with a single mast with two headsails. . . ."

"You need to speak in terms a boy can understand, Lucas. Jamie is not a sailor yet." Caroline chuckled and shook her head as father and son walked away. "I've never seen Lucas so happy. Jamie is good for him."

"I agree. For the most part, Lucas has been a somber type for as long as I've known him," Mr. Madison said.

"And how long has that been?" Heather asked, keeping her eye on Jamie and his father.

Mr. Madison looked at his wife. "What say you? Four years?"

She nodded. "We met him shortly after we bought the neighboring plantation. We call it Madison Gardens."

"Perhaps I'll get to see it before I leave," Heather said.

Caroline laid her hand on Heather's arm. "I would love that. You'll have to encourage Lucas to drive you and Amelia—that's Lucas's mother—over for tea one afternoon."

Heather couldn't help wondering how long she'd be at Reed Springs. "That sounds lovely, but I'm not sure how long it will take Mr. Reed to find a permanent governess."

"Excuse me, ladies, but I shall take my leave and join Lucas and Jamie." Mr. Madison gave a brief bow and moseyed away.

"You should probably be prepared to stay awhile. Lucas would have had far better luck at finding a governess in Charleston than he will at Reed Springs. I still think it odd that he seemed in such a hurry to return to the plantation. We weren't scheduled to leave Charleston for another week."

Heather focused again on the landscape. Mr. Reed *had* seemed quite anxious ever since the day they'd ordered clothing and had eaten at McCrady's. He'd wanted to leave that very same day, but Mr. Madison had said it would be impossible for him to go before the end of the week, and Caroline had reminded him that the clothing they'd ordered wouldn't be ready before then either. So they'd waited, but Mr. Reed hadn't seemed able to completely relax until this ship set sail. Had something happened that day?

"Perhaps he is just anxious for his mother to meet Jamie," Heather offered.

"That is probably the truth of the matter. Amelia will adore her grandson. She longs to see Lucas married and the past put behind him."

What past was she referring to? Did his mother know of his relationship with Deborah?

"Look over there." Caroline pointed to the far shore. "See that white bird?"

Heather's gaze searched the shoreline then landed on the creature. White as snow, it was. She nodded.

"It's called a snowy egret."

She studied the large bird with thin, black legs and odd yellow feet. "Why, its eyes look yellow."

"They are. Isn't that odd?"

Heather nodded and watched the bird get smaller as they moved past.

The next hour sailed by. Lucas returned with Jamie, who chattered about the various parts of the ship. Heather smiled over his head at Caroline. They returned their attention to the shoreline, playing a game of counting how many different birds they could see.

"Is that a turtle swimming over there?" Heather squinted her eyes and pointed across the sun-glistened water toward the shore.

"No!" Caroline clutched Heather's arm. "That's an alligator's head. See his wide-set eyes?"

"Where? I can't see!" Jamie tried once again to climb onto the gunwale.

Heather hauled him up into her arms, knowing she could only hold him for a few moments. When had he grown so heavy? "Right there under that branch that sticks out over the water. See it now?"

"Aye! It's so big." He put one hand on the edge of the rail and lurched forward, nearly slipping from her grasp.

Heather gasped and grabbed his pants at the waist, hauling him back. "You must be careful, lad. If you were to fall in, you might become fodder for that beast."

"Miss Hawthorne is right."

Heather jumped at the nearness of Mr. Reed's voice. She turned, and he took his son. Would he harshly scold him for his overeagerness?

Caroline left them and joined her husband, who was seated on a wooden crate, studying a paper in his hand.

"Jamie, look at me."

The lad leaned back in his father's arms and stared at him, his blue eyes filled with worry.

"You must always be careful and alert aboard ship. Accidents have killed many a good sailor. Do you understand?"

Jamie nodded his head. "Aye, aye, Captain."

Heather bit back a smile at his nautical response. Mr. Reed grinned and looked at her. Something hitched inside her as they shared their delight in the lad they both cared for. She and this colonist had something very precious in common. But soon Jamie would belong only to him. Turning around, she focused on the serene setting, shoving back her melancholy thoughts. Perhaps it would have been better had she not agreed to be Jamie's temporary governess. Jamie was adapting to his father far more easily than she'd expected. Hiking her chin, she blinked back the tears burning her eyes.

Soon he wouldn't need her at all.

❧

Holding his son's hand, Lucas guided him across the deck to where his first mate stood talking with the helmsman. "I thought Jamie might enjoy seeing below deck. Would you mind giving him a tour?"

The man nodded. " 'Twould be my pleasure, Captain."

Jamie glanced up. "Aren't you coming?"

"No, son. I need to keep an eye on things up here, and I want to have a word with your aunt Heather. You'll be safe, and you can return whenever you've seen all that you want to."

"All right."

Lucas watched the two go below deck then strode over to where Miss Hawthorne stood. She was a comely woman. Small in stature but like a she-bear when it came to defending her adopted cub. He liked the way her brown eyes snapped when she was upset and how she hiked that pert little nose in the air. In fact, the only thing he didn't like about her was that she planned to leave.

He hadn't been so attracted to a woman since Deborah. He should be interviewing for a governess instead of rushing back to Reed Springs, but ever since that woman confronted him near the docks, he'd felt an urgent need to get Jamie out of Charleston. He hoped the woman would keep silent. *Please, Lord.*

Lucas slowed his steps and approached from an angle, so as not to frighten Miss Hawthorne again. "So, what do you think of our fine country?"

She scowled but kept her focus somewhere other than on him. "I can't deny its rugged beauty. So many unusual birds and flowers."

"Wait until you see my mother's garden. You've not seen the likes of her flowers anywhere."

A soft smile tugged at her lips. "Sounds lovely. The growing season up north is so short that I crave things of beauty like flowers. I can see why you are fond of this region, although I don't know how you handle the abysmal heat."

"It can be hard at times, but we adapt. Evening events are held late, generally after the sun sets, and it's not uncommon to rest in the heat of the day." He boldly fingered the sleeve of her new day dress, causing her to look up at him. "We also wear clothing made of cooler fabrics. There are many things one can do."

She held his gaze uncommonly long. "You will be good to Jamie? You promise not to let anything happen to him?" She blinked her eyes then swatted at a tear. "I couldn't bear it."

He laid his hand over hers. "I'll do everything within my power to keep him safe. I already love him."

She continued to stare, as if measuring his sincerity, then nodded and tugged her hand out from under his. "And what of your mother? Will she accept an. . .illegitimate child?"

Ah, so that's what bothered her. He watched the black needlerush grasses swishing in the breeze. On shore, birds chirruped a chorus, and midstream, a fish leaped out of the water and then disappeared again. "Mother will adore Jamie. Her only regret will be the same as mine—that we were unable to have him sooner."

Heather stiffened, and her chin lifted. "I thought I explained that."

"You did, and I understand, but it doesn't change the fact that we missed out on years of Jamie's growth."

"Perhaps you should have thought about that before you walked out on his mother." She hung her head, as if embarrassed by her outburst. "I wasn't sure that you'd even want him at all," she whispered so softly he barely heard her.

He heaved a sigh, wishing he could tell her the whole truth. But if Deborah hadn't, then he didn't feel he should. He still didn't know whether to tell his mother or not. She would love Jamie no matter which son sired him, but the truth was he dreaded having her think less of him—that he was capable of doing such a heinous deed.

But didn't she have the right to know?

He'd better make up his mind fast, because Madison Gardens was around the next corner, and another mile down the river, Reed Springs awaited.

six

"Oh, my goodness." Heather gazed past the dock as the ship slowly veered toward it. Her first glimpse of Reed Springs all but took her breath away. A well-used path led up to a wide, green lawn, the centerpiece of which was a three-story, red brick house. This structure wasn't as ornate as the Charleston house, but its massive size made it every bit as daunting. The first level looked to be partially underground with windows that seemed to grow right out of the grass. A wide stairway led up to the second level, which she assumed was the main floor. On the sides of the massive white front doors were three widely spaced windows, also trimmed in white, and on the floor above were three larger windows in the center with two smaller ones on either side.

The ship bumped against the dock, and sailors cast heavy ropes to two Negroes on the wooden ramp. Lucas turned to Jamie. "Are you ready to see our other home, son?"

Jamie glanced at her then nodded. Lucas escorted Jamie down the gangplank then lifted his gaze to her. Heather's heart thumped. She didn't want to be attracted to him. She had despised him for years for neglecting Deborah and her son, but the man had already effectively disarmed her with his kindness.

He patted Jamie's shoulder. "Stay here, son, while I assist Miss Hawthorne down."

He jogged back up the gangplank then beckoned her to him with his fingers. She swallowed the sudden lump that had risen to her throat and reluctantly obeyed. She placed her hand in his, and he deftly helped her down the steep walkway. When they were on solid ground, he captured her gaze and continued to hold her hand. Her breath grew shaky under his intense stare. He grinned. The rogue knew the effect he had on her.

Scowling, she yanked her hand away, swept past him, and claimed Jamie's hand. How could Mr. Reed realize the effect he had on her when she barely recognized it herself? She tugged Jamie forward. "Come, you have a grandmother to meet."

❧

Lucas chuckled. *Feisty little thing, aren't you?* He shook his head. What had gotten into him?

Normally, he'd stay and see to the ship, but today he had highly important matters to attend to. He was about to give his mother the shock of her life. Nothing could please her more than a grandchild, except perhaps to see Marcus repent of his vile ways and come to know God.

Lucas found it difficult to believe his brother could ever have a change of heart, but stranger things had happened. And last time he checked, God was still in the miracle-working business. He quickened his steps and caught up with Miss Hawthorne and Jamie. She sidled a glance at him, and he couldn't miss her apprehension. "Everything will be fine. More than fine, in fact."

As they reached the stairs, Lucas slowed his pace then stopped. He turned back to face her. "Perhaps I should inform Mother about Jamie rather than shocking her with his sudden presence."

She studied him, nibbling on her lower lip in an enticing manner, then nodded. "Aye, that is probably the wise thing to do. Jamie and I can wait here."

Lucas motioned for the servant who was carrying their satchels to step forward. "Moses, let me have those bags, and take Miss Hawthorne and Jamie to the kitchen and see that they have something to drink and something to eat if they wish."

Moses seemed reluctant to turn over the bags to Lucas, but he finally relinquished them. "Thisa way, miss."

Miss Hawthorne followed the servant around the steps to a door that led below the main stairway. She glanced up at Lucas, and he smiled, hoping to reassure her that all would be well. When she disappeared under the stairs, he hurried up to the main floor of the house. He hoped his mother wasn't resting. Now that they were home, excitement thrummed through him to reveal his news to her.

In the entry, he waited a moment for his eyes to adjust to the dimmer lighting, then searched the parlor and music room but failed to find his mother. Mouthwatering scents drifted up from the kitchen, making him wonder what was for dinner. He walked to the back of the house and finally located her in the dining room, where she had covered the table with fragrant cut flowers that she was arranging in bouquets and putting into vases.

"Lucas! Thank the good Lord you've returned." She stepped back from the table and hurried forward, worry straining her still pretty face.

"What's wrong?"

She hugged him then stepped back with her hand over her heart. "We've had some thievery."

Lucas winced. He didn't like the thought of his mother alone in this big house with just a servant or two for protection. She knew how to handle a flintlock pistol, but he didn't want her placed in the position where it was necessary to use one. "When? What did they take?"

"A hen and a few tools the first night. Then two piglets several nights later."

"Hmm. . .the tools rule out the thief being an animal.

Perhaps we have some vagrants around. Have the field-workers sighted any strangers?"

She shook her head. "Not that I know of."

"Well, worry no more. I'll see to it now that I'm here."

She hugged him again. "I missed you. How long will you be home this time?"

Rubbing his chin with his thumb and index finger, he stared at her. She looked tired. Though fifty years old, and her brown hair had not yet yielded completely to the gray, she had purple smudges under her eyes. "Are you getting enough rest?"

"Of course. Our servants are so efficient that I could rest all day if I wanted."

"But you'd never do that." He smiled. "I have a surprise for you."

She glanced past him, searching, then caught his gaze. "Where is it?"

"Downstairs."

"In the kitchen?"

"Yes. But you may want to sit down and let me explain before you run down there."

She lifted her chin. "A lady never runs."

"We shall see. Please have a seat, Mother." She did as he bid then looked up with curious, blue-gray eyes. He sucked in a deep breath and exhaled. Where to begin?

With his hands clasped behind him, he paced the length of the table and back to her. "Just over a week ago, I had two visitors. A comely woman arrived at my door with a young boy in tow, claiming he was mine."

His mother's eyes widened. "How dreadful to use a child to obtain a few coins. Did you turn them out?"

"I did not. I was intrigued with the boy. He has the look of the Reed men, Mother."

"But there are many children with dark hair and blue eyes." She squeezed the stem of a flower until it broke in half.

Lucas ran his hand through his hair. If he told her about the letter from Deborah, surely his mother would figure out what happened.

"How old was the boy?"

"He's five."

She stood and walked over to him. "Then it's impossible for the child to be yours, as much as I wish it might be so. You had already become a believer in Christ by then, and I know you'd never fall into sin in such a manner."

"Thank you, Mother." She was a wise woman, his mother. He should have known he'd have to tell her the whole truth, and perhaps that was best. "He isn't mine. The boy is Marcus's son."

Her hand flew to her chest as she gazed at him with wide eyes; then she schooled her expression. "But how could you possibly know if it's true? Anybody could show up at your door and make such a claim."

"There was a letter from the boy's mother."

"And?"

He pursed his lips and strode to the window, staring out at the green lawn. The grass had been brown when he was last here. A sudden memory of walking on that lawn with Deborah assaulted him. It pained him to think of sweet, gentle Deborah enduring what she had. He felt his mother's hand on his shoulder.

"Tell me, son."

"His mother was Deborah." The words came out on a whisper.

She turned him around, her eyes filled with compassion. "Oh, Lucas. I'm so sorry." Suddenly she scowled. "How could Marcus do that to you? To Deborah? I don't want to believe him capable of such a horrible act."

"I'm sorry, Mother."

"You have nothing to be sorry for. It's not your doing."

He shook his head. "I should have searched longer for her. Looked in more places."

"No, you did far more than anyone expected. You left home, your business, and hunted for her for nearly two years. No man could have done more."

"Yet I failed."

"Shh. . .no more, I said." She patted his arm, her eyes sparking with hope. "So, it's true then? The boy is a Reed? He truly is my grandson?"

He nodded. "Jamie is his name. But there's something else. He arrived with a young woman who has raised him since Deborah died."

She gasped. "Deborah's dead?"

"Yes. Three years now. The woman's name is Miss Heather Hawthorne, and she's from Canada. Deborah told her that Jamie was *my* son."

"Why would she do such a thing?"

"To protect him. He'd be scorned all his life if people knew he was the son of the Black Mark. I've accepted Jamie as my own, and that's all anyone will ever know if I can help it."

She looked out the window, as if digesting all that he'd told her. " 'Tis a fine, honorable thing you've done, son. I know this will cause talk among our friends and neighbors and that you'll face hardship and scorn from some people because of Jamie, but I'm proud of you."

He straightened and wrapped his arm around his mother's shoulders. "Thank you. It means a lot to have your support."

She reached up and patted his cheek. "You've always had my support, son."

"There's one more thing. You need to know that Miss

Hawthorne is not aware that I have a brother, much less that he's Jamie's true father."

"Don't you think she should know the truth?"

Lucas shrugged. "If Deborah wanted her to know, don't you think she would have told her?"

"I suppose she feared word getting out about Marcus."

He pursed his lips and nodded.

"We can talk more of these things later, but now, I want to see my grandson."

Without waiting for him, she lifted up her skirts and hurried toward the staircase—not running, but almost.

❧

Heather surveyed the large kitchen while Jamie enjoyed a slice of bread with creamy butter and strawberry jam and a glass of milk. A soot-blackened brick hearth held a large cauldron of bubbling soup or stew. The pot hung on a long rod with a hook on the end so it could be pulled off the fire when done cooking. Two women worked in unison, one cutting biscuits and the other laying them on a baking pan.

Footsteps sounded on the inside stairwell, and an older woman with brownish-gray hair and sparkling eyes hurried down, her dress swishing. Mr. Reed's mother, Heather presumed. The woman's hungry gaze latched on to Jamie, who continued eating, oblivious that he had an audience. Mr. Reed arrived in the kitchen right after his mother. He walked around the table, and when Jamie spied him, the boy smiled.

"Come, son, let's clean you up. Your grandmother is eager to make your acquaintance." One of the servants scurried over with a damp cloth and wiped Jamie's hands and face. "Thank you, Mable."

The shorter of the two Negro women nodded, smiled, and returned to her worktable. Heather resisted shaking her head. Did Mr. Reed's kindness know no bounds?

"Jamie"—Mr. Reed motioned to his mother—"this is Amelia Reed, your grandmother. Mother, this is Jamie, my son."

The other servant peered over her shoulder with wide eyes before quickly turning around again. Mrs. Reed moved cautiously, as if Jamie were a butterfly she might startle away. "I'm so happy to meet you, Jamie, and am so glad that you've joined our family."

Jamie's gaze darted to Heather's, and she smiled and nodded. He gave a half bow and said, "I'm happy to meet you, too."

Mrs. Reed chuckled and ran her hand down his head. "You look like your father." She smiled at her son.

"Aye, that's what people keep saying." Jamie glanced down at his plate. "May I finish my bread now?"

"Certainly. Is there anything else you'd like?" Mrs. Reed pulled out a chair, never taking her eyes off her grandson.

"I think Jamie has had enough for now, but before you sit down, Mother, I'd like to introduce Miss Hawthorne." He leaned toward his mother, and spoke softly. "She raised Jamie after his mother died and is the one responsible for bringing him here. I've asked her to remain as Jamie's governess until I can hire a permanent one."

Mrs. Reed scurried toward her. "Please forgive my appalling manners, dear. I have no excuse except for being mesmerized with my grandson. I can never express my gratitude to you for all you've done."

"No thanks are needed, ma'am. Jamie is a good lad and a delight to care for. 'Tis a pleasure to meet you."

"And you. Why don't you have a seat and some refreshment? I know the trip here isn't overly long, but it's a warm day." Mrs. Reed gestured toward the table.

Heather smiled then took a seat across from Jamie while his grandmother slid in beside him. Mrs. Reed patted Jamie's shoulder and smiled. "God has surely blessed us this day."

seven

While his mother, Miss Hawthorne, and Jamie lingered over breakfast the next morning, Lucas strode out to the barn to investigate the thefts. Folks along the river were neighbors and most of them friends, with the exception of a few staunch Loyalist holdouts who were highly verbal about their beliefs and still swore their allegiance to England, but he couldn't imagine any of them resorting to stealing. He'd never had this problem before and wasn't sure how to handle the situation. Not only was he concerned for his mother's well-being, but now he had Jamie and Miss Hawthorne to worry about, as well.

After watching the two ladies interact with Jamie most of yesterday, he had to admit he admired Miss Hawthorne more and more. He was certain she'd done without to provide for his son and to bring him here. Whenever he thought of hiring another woman to watch Jamie, his heart clenched. He didn't want Miss Hawthorne to go.

He inspected the well-manicured flower beds and neat hedges and nodded to a couple of servants weeding the lush spring flowers as he passed by. "Well done!"

The men smiled and nodded their thanks for his appreciation. Slavery was dreadful, and he in good conscience could not abide it. Most of the older servants remained from his father's days. Even though he'd freed them, they'd stayed on, working for room and board and a fair wage, but a few newer ones he'd purchased as slaves at public auction and then set free, only to turn around and house them and pay them a wage. The expenses cut into his profit, but he was rewarded with the workers' loyalty and appreciation. God had blessed his business, and he was able to sleep at nights, knowing he'd done right by his servants, even though some of his associates scorned him for his unconventional beliefs.

He walked into the barn, wondering where his overseer was. Breathing in the familiar scents of horses, fresh hay, and leather, he searched for one of his servants. Samuel, a master with horses, stood in a stall toward the rear of the barn, humming as he brushed Lucas's horse. When Lucas walked closer, his black gelding noticed him and stuck his head over the stall and whickered.

"Whoa, hoss," Samuel said, reaching for the animal's halter.

Lucas scratched the white diamond on the gelding's forehead. "How are you, Liberty?"

"He be just fine 'n' dandy, Missah Reed. Though I 'magine he'd like a good, long run."

"Him and me both. But first I need to know if anything has been discovered about the thief."

Samuel left the stall and shook his head. "Nah, sir. Not nothin' but some footprints."

"Show me where they are."

"Well. . ." Samuel scratched his chest. "They's gone now. It done went and rained the night of that second robbery, and footprints was tracked inside the barn from all the mud, but they's good and dried up now."

Lucas scanned the barn to see if anything looked out of place. "Mother said they stole some tools."

"Just an ol' ax. I'm guessin' it was to kill that chicken they done stole."

Lucas stood with his hands on his hips, staring out the barn door. He could stand to lose a chicken to a hungry person, and even a couple of piglets, but what if the man decided he wanted a horse next time?

"Do you know where Mr. Remington is?"

"Yassah. He done went down to the fields."

Lucas didn't want to wander that far from home today in case he was needed. His mother and Jamie were getting along famously, but Miss Hawthorne seemed a bit withdrawn. Could be she was just feeling out of place or even left out since Jamie had taken so well to his grandmother's affection and pampering. If he didn't watch out, his son would soon be spoiled. Perhaps a ride out to the fields with him would be good for Jamie.

"Go ahead and saddle Liberty for me."

"You wants me to bring him up to the big house?"

"No, but thank you." Lucas studied the man who'd worked on the plantation for a good ten years. "I suppose you've heard the news that I have a son who's come to live here."

"Yassah. I think that be a blessing from God, I do."

Lucas nodded. "Me, too. If Jamie ever happens down here alone, I'd be grateful if you'd keep a good eye on him. He's not used to being around horses, and I wouldn't want anything to happen to him."

"You can count on Samuel." He smiled and nodded. "I be watchin' that boy like he's my own."

Lucas clapped the man on the shoulder. "I appreciate that, Samuel."

He started back to the house. If only things with Miss Hawthorne could go as easily as with Samuel.

❧

"I normally take a rest after luncheon, but I'm anxious to start remodeling this bedchamber for Jamie." Mrs. Reed ambled around the room. "This used to be the nursery."

Heather liked how the chamber had been refurbished and now held a double bed with a canopy and colorful floral draperies. An unusual rocking chair sat in one corner. Her gaze traveled along one arm of the chair and up and around the curved top and down to the other arm, all a single, continuous piece of wood held in place by long, decorative spindles that formed the back and sides.

Mrs. Reed lifted the edge of one drape and shook her head. "This simply will not do for a boy. I'll have to order some fabric from Charleston and have these remade."

"I'm certain Jamie won't mind things as they are now." She glanced over to where he sat in the open doorway that led to a balcony, stacking pieces of wood that looked as if they were leftover from a building project. Mrs. Reed said they used to be his father's.

What would she say if she knew her grandson had been sleeping on a simple cot, covered with ragged quilts discarded after a neighbor's fire?

Jamie was far better off here, even though he'd grow up an American. He'd have family who loved him and a good education, and he'd never lack anything. He might miss her, but his grandmother and father would give him all the love he needed.

Heather should have brought him here sooner.

If only she'd had the means.

She sighed and strolled over to the door, staring out at the expansive lawn. Sculpted bushes and flower beds ran all along the front of the house, adding color and loveliness to the brick and wrought iron.

"Well, there's nothing more to be done in here until I order some new things. Would you two care for a stroll in the garden before the temperatures warm too much?"

Heather spun around. "Aye. That would be lovely. I've been wanting to see your pretty flowers up close."

The older woman smiled. "Wonderful. I do so enjoy them,

but I much prefer to have someone else with me. And before you get your hopes up, some flowers are blooming, but it's still early, so many varieties have yet to open their faces to the sun."

Heather wondered if Mrs. Reed was lonely. Living so far from Charleston, she was all but isolated here for much of the time. She would certainly enjoy having her grandson's company.

Mrs. Reed reached out a hand to Jamie. "Come, Jamie, shall we take a walk?"

He eyed the wood pieces he'd stacked in a tall tower as if he wasn't quite ready to leave them; then he glanced at Heather.

"Those will be here when we return," she said. "You may play with them again later."

Looking a bit disappointed, Jamie stood and took his grandmother's hand. He'd always been a sweet, compliant child and rarely complained or pitched a fit. Until now, she'd assumed he had inherited such traits from his mother, but having met Mr. Reed and his mother, she was no longer so certain. Both Reeds seemed to be good-natured people with big hearts. Guilt nibbled at her for thinking so badly of them all these years. But if Mr. Reed was as good a man as he seemed, how could he have done such a deed to Deborah?

As Mrs. Reed led Jamie from the room, he reached out and took Heather's hand, too. She smiled down at him, receiving a grin from him in return. Perhaps he did still need her.

They ambled through the wide hall with its decorative ceiling, soft bluish-green walls the color of the sea, and furniture so shiny that she could see her reflection. Two chairs upholstered in ivory-colored brocade sat in a corner alcove with a potted palm tree about Jamie's height situated between them.

At the front door, Mrs. Reed took a straw hat off a

hall tree and handed Heather's to her. Once outside, they descended the front stairs into the warm sunshine. Mr. Reed met them as they reached the ground.

"Off on an outing, I presume?" he asked.

"No, son. We're simply out to take a walk in the gardens."

He eyed Heather. What could he want with her? Had he already hired a governess? She swallowed hard. Jamie was adapting well, but would he be bereft once she left? Her heart ached at the thought of causing him pain.

"I wonder if I might have a chat with Miss Hawthorne."

Mrs. Reed glanced back at her and smiled. "I suppose you should ask her. Jamie and I can stroll the garden and hunt for butterflies and bees."

Jamie scowled. "I don't like bees. They sting."

Mrs. Reed hugged the boy. "Then we shall see how many different butterflies we can find. All right?"

He nodded and waved at Heather.

"Oh my. A carriage is coming." Mrs. Reed stared down the long lane. A fine coach drawn by a pair of matched gray horses emerged from the tree line and rolled past a creek with an arched walking bridge and a pond with a white gazebo partially covered with ivy.

"Are you expecting guests, Mother?"

Mrs. Reed shook her head. "I've no idea who that could be."

Heather didn't know whether to snatch up Jamie and run back inside or stay. How would Mr. Reed explain his son—and was he ready to do so?

He stared at the carriage for a moment then turned back to his mother. "Isn't that the Duponts' carriage? I recognize the horses."

Mrs. Reed gasped and held a hand to her mouth. "What day is this?"

He lifted one dark brow. "Saturday. Why?"

"Oh dear. I'd forgotten that Gwenda and Hilary were coming to tea. They were not supposed to be here until four, though. Surely it can't be that late." She glanced at the sun. "I wonder why they are so early." Mrs. Reed squeezed her forehead. "I'm not even certain if there's anything ready to serve them."

"I'm sure there is something. Mable always has goodies of some sort available." Mr. Reed dusted the sleeves of his white shirt and tugged on the bottom of his waistcoat. "I need to fetch my frock coat. I'm not in the proper dress to receive guests."

"Would you like me to go and check with Mable about refreshments?" Heather offered.

Relief softened Mrs. Reed's face. "Oh, would you, dear?"

"I'd be happy to."

"And could you please find Mrs. Overton and have her locate Elijah, my manservant? Have him run up to my room and get my tan frock and bring it to me?" Mr. Reed's expression looked hopeful.

"Aye. My pleasure."

"Take Jamie with you." Mr. Reed reached for his son's hand and smiled. "Go inside with Miss Hawthorne, and perhaps Mable will have a treat for you."

Heather returned to the house with Jamie in tow. Had his father purposely sent them both away? Was he ashamed of Jamie?

She hurried through the house, searching for the housekeeper, but had no luck finding her. Even though she'd offered her assistance, she couldn't help feeling as if Mr. Reed hadn't wanted the guests to meet Jamie. She shook her head, scolding herself for her negative thinking. Perhaps he simply wanted to prepare them first. When she didn't find the housekeeper, she scurried downstairs to the kitchen with

Jamie following. Should she return out front after finding out if there were any cakes to serve with the tea?

Mable was alone today, but she smiled as they entered. "They's that fine, young gent'aman."

Jamie smiled. "Father said I might have a treat."

"Did he now?"

"Indeed." Jamie climbed onto a chair at the worktable. "What kind of treats you got?"

"Have, Jamie. What kind of treats do you have?" Heather smoothed his hair and tucked in his shirt.

"That's what I said."

Mable giggled. "I has some scones and strawberries or some o' them little cakes you'uns had yesterday at tea."

"Mmm, I want the cakes." Jamie bounced on the chair.

"Before you give him that, I need to inform you that Mrs. Reed has guests who are just arriving."

Mable nodded and stirred something in a pot over the fire. A delicious scent filled the air. "Mmm-huh. She done told me last week that they's a'comin'. But I thought they was comin' later in the afternoon."

"I think they were supposed to, but they're here now. Mrs. Reed said something about them being early."

"Humph. That Miss Hilary, she likes to make a scene. She gots her cap set for Mr. Lucas if you ask me." Mable brought over a plate with two small cakes and set them before Jamie.

Heather's heart skipped a few beats. Miss Dupont had designs on Mr. Reed? What would that mean for Jamie? What did it mean for her?

Heather's hands tightened on the back of Jamie's chair. If Mr. Reed were to marry, his new wife might be cruel to Jamie or send him away altogether once she had her own children.

Heavy footsteps and a metallic jingling sounded on the

stairs, and a flash of black skirt showed as the housekeeper stepped into the room. "We've guests. Make haste, Mable."

The cook set a teapot onto the fire. "The wata' is heatin' and the scones is made."

"Ah, very good." Mrs. Overton's shoulders lowered as she relaxed.

Heather approached the housekeeper. "Mr. Reed asked me to have you find Elijah and have him collect Mr. Reed's tan frock coat from his bedchamber and take it to him. He was outside in front of the house a few moments ago."

"Ach! That man. Don't know why he can't take his coat when he leaves the house." The tall, thin woman spun around, and hiking up her skirt, dashed up the stairs. The clinking of the numerous keys hanging from her chatelaine could be heard until she reached the second floor.

Mable shook her head. "That woman, she's more flighty than a nest of spooked pheasants." She shook her head and laid a half dozen scones on an etched silver tray. She removed a shiny silver teapot from a shelf and set it on the table.

Heather giggled at the woman's bluster. She'd been around a few slaves, and the servants at Reed Springs were little like them. Slaves tended to keep their heads down and never looked a white man in the eye or sassed him. The servants here had more spunk and seemed happy and content. Just one more thing that elevated Lucas Reed in her mind.

eight

Lucas slipped his arms into his coat and straightened it just as the carriage made its final turn. "Elijah, please inform Mrs. Overton that we'll take refreshments in the parlor as soon as our guests are settled."

"I'll see to it, sir."

"Thank you." He nodded.

His mother leaned toward him. "What do we tell them about Jamie?"

A myriad of thoughts raced through his mind. Hilary Dupont was the last person he'd expected to see today. The pretty but chatty woman had long ago set her cap for him, even though he'd offered no encouragement. He hadn't been interested in making a match with a woman since he'd lost Deborah. But if he was being completely honest, of late his desire to settle down had been stirred up by a shy northerner. What he needed to figure out was if that desire was birthed from gratitude because Miss Hawthorne had brought Jamie to him—or if it was the woman herself who intrigued him.

He refocused on the carriage as it slowed. He'd hoped for a week alone with his mother before he had to introduce Jamie to any friends or neighbors. If Hilary knew, it wouldn't be long before everyone along the Ashley River did, and guests would be arriving in droves to hear how it all had come about.

Sooner or later, everyone would know anyway. Wouldn't it be better if he was the one who first delivered the news to Hilary? At least there'd be less spurious blather that way.

The carriage rolled to a halt, and Lucas stiffened his spine.

He could only pray for a brief visit. Normally, he'd offer his greetings and take his leave after a short while, but with Jamie here, he didn't want to leave his mother at the mercy of the two Dupont women, who would pry and prod until they'd revealed every sordid detail. He loved his mother, but she could never keep a secret. The last thing he wanted was for people to know Jamie was Deborah's child. Or Marcus's.

He opened the carriage door and forced a smile. "Good afternoon, ladies."

"Why, Mr. Reed, what a lovely surprise to see you." Hilary smiled and reached for his hand, and he helped her disembark. Her silver and lavender skirts rustled as she stepped as close as her petticoats would allow. An overpowering floral scent permeated the air, putting him in mind of a walking lilac bush.

"I thought you weren't expected to return until next week." She batted her thick lashes. The beguiling look in her unusual, near-violet eyes made him wonder if she'd known he was home and that was why she was here now. Had word already gotten out about Jamie?

"I decided to return sooner than planned," he said.

Hilary's mother was just as bold in her stare. Both women had made it clear that they intended to see Hilary married to him, but he'd rather be keelhauled. Still, he would be the polite host and hope they'd soon lose interest in making him their quest and focus on some other prey.

"Welcome." His mother stepped forward. "It's so good to see you both. Shall we go inside where it's cooler?"

Mrs. Dupont nodded and fluttered her fan. "Dreadfully hot for so early in the day, is it not? You needn't have waited outside for us, Amelia."

"Oh, but I was about to take a stroll in the garden with—"

"Mother, perhaps the conversation could wait until we're

inside and we've made our guests comfortable?" Lucas despised interrupting her, but he wanted control of any talk of Jamie. He offered his arm to both older women, helping them up the stairs and effectively holding Hilary at bay.

"Of course," his mother responded. "Do let us retire from this heat."

In the parlor, Mrs. Dupont sat on the sofa while Hilary situated herself on the narrower canapé, leaving room on the end, no doubt, for him. Resisting Hilary's unspoken invitation, he strode to the fireplace and rested his elbow on the mantel.

"How is the shipping business these days?" Mrs. Dupont asked.

"Fine. We've been blessed with clear weather for the past few weeks and have accomplished much." He bided his time until the chitchat died away. Suddenly, he straightened. Would knowing about Jamie dissuade Hilary from her mission to ensnare him as her husband?

If it did, then he was correct about the woman. But if not. . .

"And how is Howard these days?" his mother asked.

Mrs. Dupont pursed her lips. "Oh, you know men and their politics. He's working hard to see that South Carolina ratifies the Constitution. He's certain it will be the demise of us all if we don't. They need a majority of nine colonies, you know."

His mother waved her hand in the air. "I know nothing of such things. I leave all that to Lucas." She glanced at him and lifted her brows, as if asking, *When*?

He knew how eager she was to share Jamie with her friends. There was no point in delaying things. It would go as it would go, but he had the distinct feeling that neither of the Dupont women would take the surprise of his son well. He pushed away from the wall. Hilary smiled and scooted her skirts closer to her in an open invitation for him to sit beside her. Mrs. Overton strolled in, carrying the teapot, followed by Mable, who held a tray of scones. "Mrs. Overton, where are Miss Hawthorne and Jamie?" Lucas asked.

"In the kitchen, sir. Shall I send them up?"

Lucas nodded. "Please do."

Hilary turned curious eyes upon him, as did her mother. When the servants left, he cleared his throat and plunged forward. "I had a rather startling surprise arrive while I was last in Charleston. A woman came to my door with a young boy in tow."

Hilary cast an odd glance at her mother, while his mother sat on the edge of her seat, obviously anxious.

"As it turns out, the boy is a Reed. I received documentation proving it, and I've claimed him as my son."

Hilary gasped and bounced up, her silk skirts swishing. "But—but you can't. I mean how can you possibly be certain the child is yours?"

"Just wait until you see him, and you'll understand. Jamie is a miniature of his father." His mother's warm smile revealed the love she already felt for her grandson.

Hilary flitted to the doorway and back. "You must be wrong."

"There is no doubt in my mind."

She flicked open a fan that hung by a cord around her wrist and waved it vigorously in front of her reddened face. "Who is the mother? Why have we not heard about this—this child before now?"

"Because I did not know about him until just last week."

Mrs. Dupont's fan snapped open and joined her daughter's, flapping like a pair of hummingbird wings. "This is highly irregular, Lucas. Why are you willing to take in the urchin when you weren't married to his mother?" Her cheeks paled suddenly. "You *weren't* married, were you?"

Lucas straightened, and his eyes narrowed. This woman would rather he fathered an illegitimate child than have married the boy's mother? He knew the Duponts were shallow, but he never expected them to be so coldhearted toward a child.

"Of course he wasn't married." His mother twisted her hands in her lap. "Oh dear, that didn't sound quite right. Lucas is a different man than he was when he was younger. We've all made mistakes in the past."

Lucas paced across the room then realized that brought him closer to Miss Dupont, so he strode to the front window and looked out. "Thank you, Mother, for defending me, but it isn't necessary, and Jamie is not a mistake."

A very unladylike snort erupted from Hilary's direction. "You will have a difficult time finding a woman to marry if you take in that—"

Lucas spun around and cut off her last word with a glare.

"Now, Hilary," Mrs. Dupont said. "Let's not make a mountain out of a molehill. Do come sit down."

The young woman returned his stare with her nose in the air. With a flick of her hand, she closed the fan, sashayed back to the canapé, and gracefully lowered herself onto the cushions. "When will we meet this *boy*?"

He cared not for her snide tone. How could he ever have looked twice at this woman? Aye, she was lovely on the outside, but she was like a potato whose perfect outward appearance hid a black and rotted interior. So different from Miss Hawthorne, whose love and devotion for a child that wasn't hers compelled her to travel more than a thousand miles to bring him to his father. "Any moment now. I asked the housekeeper to send him and Miss Hawthorne up."

"And just who is this Miss Hawthorne?" Mrs. Dupont asked.

Lucas straightened under her glare. "She's the woman who brought my son to me in Charleston.

Hilary narrowed her eyes at him. "How can you be certain *she* isn't the child's real mother and just trying to make a quick buck by pawning her illegitimate child off on you?"

❧

Heather held on to Jamie's shoulder, refusing to let him enter the parlor until the negative remarks died down. How could these women consider themselves friends and ask such atrocious questions? Why, it almost sounded like a wife quizzing her husband about his illegitimate son. But what gave them that right? Did Mr. Reed have an understanding with Miss Dupont?

Her heart twisted. Why should she care if he had given his affections to another woman? He was perfectly within his rights to do so. She was only concerned for Jamie.

"I have a letter from his mother stating the facts. I'll not have you slander Miss Hawthorne's reputation. She's a kind, generous woman."

"Indeed."

Though Heather couldn't see who spoke last, she thought the voice sounded as if it may have belonged to the younger woman.

"Have you considered how taking in this child might damage your reputation?"

Heather nearly gasped. She had wondered the same thing after she'd gotten to know Mr. Reed better, but for a guest in his home—especially a female guest—to voice such a thing. . . why, it simply wasn't done.

"My son is more important to me than my reputation."

Jamie glanced up at her and grinned. She cupped his cheek with her hand and smiled back, sincerely hoping he didn't fully understand the nature of the conversation.

"Without a good reputation, what future will your son have?"

Heather was certain Mr. Reed must have some kind of relationship with these women for them to speak so candidly.

A long moment of silence reigned, and Jamie started fidgeting. Could he sense the tension in the room?

"I shall go see what's keeping them."

Heather stiffened as Mr. Reed strode out of the parlor and all but collided with her. His gaze captured hers, asking how much she'd heard. His lips pursed, and she wondered if he was upset with her for eavesdropping or angered by the Duponts' bluntness. She leaned toward him. "We were waiting for. . .um. . .the heat of the conversation to die down."

He stared for a moment then nodded. "I'm sorry you had to hear all that." He squatted down in front of Jamie. "Ready to meet some of our neighbors and my mother's friends?"

Jamie nodded and released her hand.

His mother's friends. Not his? "I shall wait here until you're finished with him." Heather glanced around for a place to sit.

"No, I want you to come, too."

He held her gaze again. Her heart thudded hard. "Why do you need *me*?"

"I could use your support." He transferred Jamie's hand to his right hand and held out his elbow.

Heather stared at it, warmed and surprised by his offer to escort her when she was but a servant. She shook her head. "It wouldn't be right for me to enter on your arm, although I thank you for the offer. I'm a servant, and we don't want to give your neighbors the wrong idea."

His lips tightened, and a bit of the light drained from his eyes, but he nodded. "We shall talk about that later."

He led Jamie into the parlor, but Heather halted in the doorway. What was there to talk about?

Two finely dressed women sat stiff and unwelcoming. Their eyes latched onto Jamie. The young woman's gaze jerked up to inspect Heather. She was a beautiful woman with blond hair the color of flax piled atop her head in a becoming manner and unusual eyes that looked deep blue with a touch of purple. Perhaps her lovely lavender dress was reflected in her eyes. Everything about this woman spoke of wealth and quality. Even Heather's new day dress paled in comparison to Miss Dupont's. She shifted her feet, uncomfortable with the young woman's stare. Why should this stranger be so interested in her?

The older woman wore a day dress of pale blue that complimented her medium brown hair and blue eyes. She continued to watch Jamie, although rather than pleased with the boy, she looked. . .saddened. Had Jamie's arrival spoiled her plans for her daughter?

Mrs. Reed patted the sofa. "Jamie, come and sit by me. Miss Hawthorne, won't you have a seat? I want to introduce you to our neighbors to the northwest, the Duponts. Gwenda and Hilary live at the Magnolia Mist plantation."

Heather perched on the edge of the nearest chair and received their cold stares without flinching.

"Miss Hawthorne was so kind to bring Jamie to us. I can't tell you how wonderful it is to have a grandson. I feel as if I'm in the springtime of my life again." She kissed Jamie's head. He stared into his lap, his cheeks turning crimson. "He's such a dear boy, and can't you see how much he resembles his father?"

"Indeed." Miss Dupont flipped open a lavender fan that matched her dress and waved it in front of her face. "Do you plan to reside long at Reed Springs, Miss Hawthorne?"

Before she could answer, Mr. Reed said, "That remains unsettled. I've asked Miss Hawthorne to stay and serve as

Jamie's governess to ease his transition into our family."

"I see." Miss Dupont's lips looked as if she'd sucked on a lemon. "And where do you hail from, Miss Hawthorne?"

"England, originally." Heather was purposely vague.

"So, where do your loyalties lie? With England or America?"

Heather didn't miss the woman's challenge, but she wasn't going to fall into her trap. She lifted her chin. "With Jamie."

A small smile lifted one corner of Miss Dupont's mouth as if saying *touché*.

"But surely you must have strong ties to England."

She shook her head, realizing the truth. England meant little to her now. Everything she cared about was here. "Not any longer."

Mrs. Dupont turned her attention to Jamie. "So, what do you think about your new home?"

Jamie shrugged and toed the carpet with his shoe. He wasn't one to be shy with family, but he generally became quiet around strangers.

"Have you started learning your letters? Do you enjoy walking on stilts? Surely there's something special you enjoy."

He glanced at Heather then his father. "Papa's going to teach me to ride, and he showed me where he builds ships."

Heather's heart lurched. She watched Mr. Reed to see his reaction to being called *Papa* for the first time.

He blinked his eyes several times and actually looked stunned just before he regained his composure. "That's right, I plan to teach him to ride."

"He's too young for that, Lucas." His mother gazed up, concern tightening her lips.

"I beg to differ, Mother, but he is not. I've been riding since I was three."

She shook her head. "I didn't like your father putting you

tiny boys on those big horses. I was so afraid you'd fall off and get hurt."

Mr. Reed smiled. "We did a time or two until we learned to hold on."

His mother shook her head. "Men and their ideas. It's a wonder that any child lives long enough to grow up."

"I'm sure he will do fine," said Mrs. Dupont. "Boys adapt to physical activities far more quickly and easily than girls."

"Really, Mother, a girl could learn to ride just as easily as a boy if she had the proper instruction." Miss Dupont patted her hair and smiled. "I was wondering, Lucas, if I might have a moment of your time to discuss an important matter."

A muscle twitched in his jaw as he coolly stared at her. The difference in their behavior confused Heather. Miss Dupont referred to Mr. Reed by his Christian name and seemed highly familiar with him, while he was more reserved, tense, and withdrawn. "I suppose that can be arranged. We can step into the music room if you'd like."

She arose, regal like a princess, and strutted toward him with a beguiling smile on her face. Glaring at Heather, she looped her arm through Mr. Reed's without his offering it to her, then tugged him out of the room. At the doorway, he stopped suddenly. "Miss Hawthorne, would you be so kind as to serve as chaperone?"

Heather's mouth went dry. She was glad to see the snippety woman leave the room, and she had no desire to follow them—although she was uncomfortable with the two of them being alone together. What if Miss Dupont said something about Jamie? She rose.

Jamie shot to his feet, a hopeful gleam in his eyes. "Might I come, too, Aunt Heather?"

"You must ask your grandmother."

He spun to face her. "May I go?"

Mrs. Reed smiled and laid her hand against his cheek. "I don't suppose an active boy like you wants to listen to two old women's prattle. You run along, and I shall see you later."

"Really, Lucas, I wanted to speak to you in private."

"Perhaps a walk in the garden would work better," he said. "That way Miss Hawthorne and Jamie can chaperone us from afar."

"I hardly think it's necessary for those two to oversee us. It's not as if I intend to take liberties with you."

Mr. Reed narrowed his eyes then lifted one brow as if remembering a time Miss Dupont had done that very thing. Heather couldn't help wondering if the woman *had* pressed her interest on him at one time or another. He moved a step ahead of Heather and glanced back over his shoulder at her, his expression imploring her to follow. She wanted to go along as little as Miss Dupont desired her to, but if her presence made Mr. Reed more comfortable, she'd go. Taking Jamie's hand, she followed them to the door. Just before she went outside, she heard Mrs. Dupont say, "Really, Amelia. You must get rid of that girl as soon as possible. As far-fetched as it sounds, she's turning Lucas's eye away from Hilary, and we can't. . ."

She closed the door, not hearing the final words. Surely the woman was mistaken. Mr. Reed had never shown the slightest interest in her. He was simply being kind because that was his nature. Yet didn't his gaze linger a bit longer than was necessary at times? And his hands had prolonged contact when he'd helped her down from the ship the day they arrived. Why would he take a second look at her—an *Englishwoman* with no dowry—when he could have the lovely Miss Dupont by his side?

What stuff and nonsense.

nine

Lucas escorted Miss Dupont down the front stairs and into the garden. A variety of flowers had already opened up and filled the air with their sweet scent. Butterflies flitted from bloom to bloom, peaceful and quiet, soothing his irritation. He'd known some of his friends and acquaintances would question if he was doing the right thing by taking in Jamie, but his heart indeed confirmed that he was. He'd already grown to love the boy.

Hilary glanced over her shoulder, staring back at Miss Hawthorne and Jamie, where they lingered at the beginning of the garden. She edged closer to him. "Really, Lucas, I don't see why you had to insist we have a chaperone."

"We wouldn't want tongues wagging now, would we?"

"Just what do you think will happen when word gets out about that boy living here? Why couldn't you board him in some school and provide for him that way? Why is it necessary to bring him into your home?"

He stopped and turned to face her, causing her to release his arm. "Because he's a Reed."

"He's a—"

"Hold your tongue, woman. That's my son you're referring to." Lucas had never held a special interest for Miss Dupont, other than to admire her beauty, as did every other man she encountered. He thought her a silly girl, somewhat younger than he, and found her efforts to snag him for a husband humorous. Until today, he hadn't realized what a vixen she was.

She stomped her foot. "I won't let that. . .that. . .*boy* come between us. When we marry, *our* children will be your rightful heirs, not that—"

Lucas held up his hand. "You forget yourself, madam. How is it you remember me proposing when I have not done so?"

Her eyes turned pleading, and her cheeks a bright red. She stuck out her lower lip in a pout that he assumed other men found enchanting, but the effort was wasted on him. "Everyone knows we have an understanding."

He quirked a brow. "Everyone but me, it would seem. I never said or did anything that should lead you to believe I wanted to marry you. I don't know that I'll ever marry."

She clutched his arm. "But you must. You can't leave all your wealth for that scoundrel brother of yours to inherit. I could give you a son, many rightful sons. Don't you know that I love you?"

Lucas heaved a sigh. He'd never been quite sure if Hilary Dupont was an innocent, spoiled woman or if she was crafty and sly. At the social events he'd attended, he noticed she often used her beauty and flirtatious ways to get the man she had designs on to lavish his attentions on her. He'd never succumbed to her childish games, but had she somehow gotten the impression that he had? *Heavenly Father, how do I get out of this without wounding her deeply?*

He cleared his throat. "I ask your forgiveness if I gave you the wrong impression, Miss Dupont. I never committed to marry you and am sorry if I did anything that implied I wanted to. I'm sure in time you will find a worthier man on whom to bestow your devotion."

Her blue eyes flashed. "Surely you know our mothers have had an arrangement since we were children. Everyone expects that we will marry."

He shook his head, more than a little confused. "How is it everyone but me understands this?"

"Because you're a stubborn buffoon who can't appreciate the woman right in front of your eyes."

Not true. His gaze darted to Miss Hawthorne. Now *there* was a woman he appreciated. From her sweet nature to her love for Jamie to her intriguing brown eyes.

"Not *her*. I meant me. How can you prefer that English trollop over a woman of my standing? How do you know the boy isn't really hers and she's just trying to pawn him off as yours to worm her way into your money box? All because he has the same coloring as you?"

Lucas stepped back as if slapped. "Woman, you forget yourself. Do not impose on my hospitality by slandering the very woman who had the gumption to travel a thousand miles to bring Jamie to me. I'll not have you belittle her."

"Humph!" Miss Dupont flung her head sideways, lifting her chin. "I see. Well, I shan't waste anymore time in a place where I'm not welcome. I shall turn my attentions elsewhere, and I shall see that my father no longer does business with you."

She swirled around and marched away, her lavender skirts swaying back and forth like a bell. As she passed a rosebush, a gust of warm wind blew, snagging the fabric. She halted, shrieked a noise that put Lucas in mind of a pig squeal, and yanked her skirt. A ripping sound made her gasp. She flung a wounded look his way then stomped toward the garden entrance.

Miss Hawthorne noted her coming and moved Jamie to her other side and out of her way. Hilary halted, said something that made Miss Hawthorne go pale, then stomped up the stairs and back into the house.

Miss Hawthorne cast a glance at him, said something to Jamie, then dashed off toward the pond. His son strolled toward him, looking concerned.

What in the world had that woman said?

❧

Heather had never before been so insulted. A hussy, indeed. And the word Miss Dupont had called Jamie—why she'd never heard a woman utter such vile accusations. What had Mr. Reed said to cause that woman to turn fangs on her?

She marched toward the pond and past it to the charming arched bridge that spanned the wide creek, trying to shake her irritation and embarrassment. Atop the bridge, she halted, staring into the water. Recent flower blossoms, which had yielded to new spring leaves, floated along on the slow current, stealing away some of her anger. A turtle sitting on a rock near the shore basked in the warm sunlight. Being able to walk around outside in April without a cloak was a delight. If only she could enjoy it.

She heaved a heavy sigh. Clearly that woman thought Heather was Jamie's mother and that she was lying about Lucas being the father. Miss Dupont said she was a swindler, stealing from the Reeds. Tears formed in Heather's eyes, blurring the lovely view, but she blinked them away.

That woman had no idea how much it had cost her to bring Jamie here. He was the only person she had left in her life. Her mother was gone, and now her father. Without Jamie, she'd be alone. Completely alone.

She sucked in a sob. She couldn't—she wouldn't—think about that now.

Jamie was still a part of her life for the time being, and she'd enjoy every moment.

In the back of her mind, a voice whispered, *He could have been yours alone if you hadn't been so honorable. His father never would have known about him. You could have kept him.*

She swatted the air, chasing away a mosquito and her wayward thoughts. Too late for such shameful regrets. Jamie would have a better life here, and hers would be better just knowing he was well cared for and loved.

If only there was someone who loved *her*.

She stood for a while, enjoying the beauty of the serene setting and allowing the peacefulness to calm her worries. The trees swayed on the light breeze, flies buzzed past her, flowers of red, purple, white, and yellow dotted the shore like an artist's palette. Birds peeped above her head, and across the bank about fifteen feet downstream, a huge spider had spun a massive web that stretched between two trees and glimmered in the sunlight.

All she had to do was not think of the day she and Jamie would be parted, and she could bear it.

Footsteps echoed beside her on the bridge, but she kept her focus forward. She wanted to be alone, but she was shirking her duties. If she didn't tend Jamie, some other servant would have to abandon her own duties to watch him.

Mr. Reed stopped beside her. His large hands grasped the top of the bridge, and he stared out at the water as she did. "It's beautiful here this time of year, is it not?"

She held her tongue, halfway afraid of what she might say. At least he hadn't come here to scold her.

He heaved a loud sigh and hung his head. "For whatever Miss Dupont said to you, I sincerely apologize."

" 'Tis not your place to express regret on her part."

"No, but she is our guest and had no right spewing her anger on you."

Again, Heather wondered what had passed between the two to make the woman lash out as she had. Could they have had a lover's quarrel? Had the woman said something as vile about Jamie to Mr. Reed as she'd spoken to her?

He glanced over his shoulder and back in the direction of the house. Anyone looking out the front parlor window could surely see them together. He straightened and pointed to the far side of the bridge. "Have you ever ventured down that path?"

"Nay." She shook her head. "After your mention of alligators, I was afraid to take Jamie anywhere near the wooded areas or ponds."

"Would you walk with me? I have some things to discuss with you."

She glanced up. Had he already found a replacement for her? Had he changed his mind about keeping Jamie in the face of his friend's outburst?

She was half afraid to agree, but she had no choice. For now, he was her employer. "Aye," she all but whispered.

He smiled and held out his elbow. "Shall we?"

She hesitated touching him. If doing so affected her as much as his smile, she was in big trouble. She couldn't afford to harbor feelings for her employer.

Still, he might be offended if she refused his escort, and spurned men often heaped their anger on the women who rebuffed them.

His dark brows rose, and his friendly blue eyes glimmered with humor. "Really, Miss Hawthorne, is it such a difficult decision to accept my arm?"

Smiling inwardly at his chivalry, she forced her hand around his warm, well-muscled arm. It was not the limb of a man from the city.

They walked along in silence, and a warm shiver wiggled down her spine when he didn't force her to talk. Birds chirped in the trees above them, and spots of sunlight broke through the heavy canopy of leaves, dappling the ground. The well-used dirt path wound through a grove of trees lining the creek, then opened up to a fenced pasture where more than a dozen horses grazed. Several foals frolicked in the knee-high grasses, kicking their awkward legs and chasing each other, while others nestled in the tall grasses, sleeping next to their grazing mothers. Nearby, a solid brown foal with a fuzzy black mane and tail nursed while its patient mother dozed. Heather's cheeks flamed, and she tried not to watch. As a young girl, she'd often slipped down to her father's stables to see the young horses come springtime, but viewing such with a gentleman present. . .

Thankfully, Mr. Reed continued to meander down the path without commenting. As they neared the end of the fence, he finally stopped and released her. She leaned against the wooden rails and continued to watch the horses, the birds, the flowers. Anything but him.

She held tight to the weathered wood, hoping to stem her nervousness. Her feelings were changing. She'd come to America a staunch British Loyalist who despised the colonists for what they'd done, but she realized now they were just people fighting for what they felt was rightfully theirs. She could understand why they wanted freedom from a ruler an ocean away who didn't understand the plight they faced in this wild land. And if she faced the truth, America's War for Independence wasn't responsible for her father losing his wealth as much as was his lust for gambling. She didn't want to believe him capable of such a deed, so she had blamed the faceless colonists.

But now they had faces—and names.

Mr. Reed paced the grass beside her with his hands locked behind his back. Whatever he wanted to talk to her about must be difficult. Why else would he be so anxious? She swallowed hard, hoping he wouldn't send her packing.

He cleared his throat. "Again, I want to express my apologies for Miss Dupont's lack of self-control. You don't need to tell me what she said. I could see that it bothered you immensely. She can be. . .um. . .overly feisty at times."

"Don't you mean rude?" Too late, she realized she'd voiced the words out loud.

He chuckled. "That, too." He stopped beside her and leaned his hip against a fence rail, staring in her direction.

She glanced sideways at him, caught his intense gaze, then smiled and looked away. *Oh my.* Did he have any idea how he affected her?

She tightened her grip on the fence, wincing as a splinter from the dried wood pricked her hand. She simply must put a stop to such nonsensical thoughts.

"I was wondering. . ."

She peered sideways, watching him fidget. Why was he nervous?

ten

Heather held her breath. The next words he uttered could mean joy or utter sadness.

"I mean," Mr. Reed said, "would you consider staying longer? I haven't had a chance to interview anyone for the governess position, and now that we're here at the plantation, I don't anticipate being able to easily interview prospects. I just think it would be best for Jamie if you could stay longer." He ran his hands through his thick, black hair and heaved another deep sigh, as if the words rushing out of him had left him breathless.

Heather's pulse increased. She could have more time with Jamie.

But then it skidded to a halt. Wouldn't that make the separation harder for him in the long run?

"Miss Hawthorne—Heather—please look at me."

Startled by his use of her Christian name, she turned toward him. His lovely eyes roved her face, making it hard for her to breathe. He tucked a strand of hair behind her ear.

"Can you deny that there is something growing between us?"

He felt it, too? She wasn't just imagining the impossible or letting her emotions run wild? She tried to swallow, but her throat felt too dry.

"I know this is an awkward situation, but I want you to know that I've not felt a thing for another woman since I lost Deborah—not until you burst into my life."

"But what of Miss Dupont? She seems to believe that you and she have an understanding."

He harrumphed and crossed his arms. "She is mistaken. I've never given her reason to assume such a thing and told her so not half an hour ago."

He cared nothing for Miss Dupont? A smile tickled her lips, and she ducked her head, ashamed at her unbridled joy.

"So, my question remains: Do you have any interest in staying longer not just for Jamie's sake, but to see if this"—he waved his hand in the air—"attraction, or whatever it is we are sensing, has any merit?"

She wanted to give free rein to her excitement, but common sense pulled back on the lines. He was as much a nobleman as you'd find in this new country, so why would he be infatuated with a poor soap maker?

Somehow, even though it might break her heart, she had to make him see reason. "I fear you've already weakened your standing among your friends and associates by agreeing to raise Jamie. How would they feel if you were to associate with a British citizen?"

He shrugged. "I have done far worse, I can assure you. And if I recall, you're now a Canadian." An enticing smirk danced on his lips.

"You may call a mule a horse, but that doesn't make it so."

"Bah! Do not belittle yourself like that." He stepped closer. "When I look at you, I see a lovely woman with beguiling brown eyes, who left her home and ventured on a long, dangerous journey to unite a young boy with his family. You're sweet and generous, and it would be my honor to have you walk at my side."

"You're too kind, sir." Tears stung her eyes as she stared at the tiny white flowers at their feet. No man had ever stood up for her, not even her father. She didn't deserve someone like Mr. Reed, not that he'd offered marriage, but she knew if they started on this course that well could be where it led. A thought burst into her mind. If she married Mr. Reed, she would be Jamie's mother!

But she couldn't do that—marry the father for the lad's sake.

Something suddenly shoved her hard in the back, forcing her forward and against Mr. Reed. His arms encircled her, and he chuckled. "It seems someone else took offense to your mule reference."

She glanced over her shoulder into a horse's muzzle. The animal blew warm breath against her face and pulled its head back to its side of the fence. She squealed and buried her cheek against her employer's waistcoat. His torso vibrated with his laughter. Realizing the impropriety of where she stood, she pushed against his chest, but the hands clutched behind her back refused to yield.

"You have not yet answered me." His eyes blazed like blue fire.

Oh, could this really be happening to her? Was he simply toying with her?

"I see a battle going on in that pretty head of yours. Have I made a dreadful assumption?" His smile disappeared, and he let go so fast she stumbled. "Do you feel nothing for me?"

"Nay."

He scowled, disappointment clouding his eyes.

"I mean nay to the first question."

He blinked, relaxing his stance. "Which question was that?"

"I, too, have felt an. . .attraction. . .to you." Her cheeks flamed. Never had she talked with a man in such a manner. "I would like to stay. . .to see what happens."

His wide smile was her reward. He ran a finger down her cheek, his eyes filling with tenderness.

"Fate has blessed me this day," she said.

He shook his head. "Not fate. God is the one who preordained it all."

She frowned. "God has never been so inclined to bless me

before. I fear He has all but turned His back on me."

"I believed that once, too. After I lost Deborah, I tried to drown out my sorrows with ale, but it never worked. I'd sober up then try it all over again. I couldn't understand why God would allow something to happen to such a gentle soul like Deborah. Until you arrived, I never knew if she'd decided marriage to me was too unbearable and ran away, or if something more nefarious had happened to her." He shook his head. "I'd be lying if I said I understand it all now, but I'm beginning to see God had a greater plan."

"Why would He allow Deborah to suffer so? After Jamie was born, she was so weak and fragile that she could hardly hold and enjoy him."

He ran his hand down the back of her head, sending delicious chills up and down her spine. "I don't know. But I can tell you that after searching for her for almost two years and not finding even a hint of where she might be, I finally reached the keel—my lowest point. A kind clergyman found me passed out in a filthy alley in Boston, took me in, and poured God's Word into me instead of ale. He helped me to see that I was a sinner loved by God but in need of repentance, just like the rest of mankind. The day I gave my heart to God, everything changed. I became a new man."

Heather pondered his words. Her mother had been a devout believer in God but not her father. After her mother died, her father never let her attend church again.

"Come, we should be getting back." He took her hand, guiding her onto the path. "As much as I wish it wasn't so, I've guests to attend, and I'm sure Jamie thinks we've abandoned him by now."

She felt almost as if they were a couple, but she didn't dare get her hopes up. What if Mr. Reed grew tired of her? Would he cast her aside?

She realized just how little she actually knew about the man. But one thing she was certain of, though he'd once been a rogue, Lucas Reed was now an honorable man. He'd certainly done right by his son.

"Do you suppose you could call me Lucas when we're alone?"

She stopped, surprised by his soft-spoken request. "You're my employer. It would hardly seem proper."

"Heather, I'd like to be a lot more than just your employer. Would it help if I were to fire you and allow you to remain here as a guest of the family?"

A smile tugged at her lips. "Nay. That isn't necessary."

He ran his knuckle across her cheek. "I love your name."

A breath caught in her throat. "Thank you."

"When we're alone, will you please call me by my Christian name?"

She ducked her head, still unsure.

With one long finger under her chin, he lifted it so that she had to look at him. "Please?"

With a resolved sigh, she nodded. "Aye. . .Lucas."

His whole face lit up with his wide grin. Curving her hand around his arm, he led her back toward the bridge, whistling a jolly tune.

❧

"You sure seem happy this morning, Lucas. Almost giddy, if you ask me, especially considering what happened yesterday."

"I do feel quite well today." Lucas glanced across the breakfast table and met his mother's curious gaze. "I'm sorry for upsetting your friends, Mother, but Miss Dupont needed to know that I'm not the man for her."

His mother stirred her tea. "I suppose I've known for a long while that you only look upon her as a neighbor and possibly a friend."

He lifted a brow. Hilary surely would no longer consider him a friend. He couldn't help wondering what kind of backlash he'd receive from rejecting her affections. The Dupont women had wide circles of influence. Well, no matter. His affections lay elsewhere, so there was nothing to be done about it. He slathered twice as much jam as normal on his bread in his effort not to look at Heather. Keeping his attraction to her under control in front of his astute mother would be difficult, but he must give Heather as much time as she needed to get to know him—and to fall in love. For he had little doubt that's where their relationship was headed.

"And what do you plan to do today, young man?"

While his mother's gaze was directed at Jamie, he peeked at Heather and winked. Her eyes widened, and her cheeks turned bright red. He bit back a grin. Teasing her and flirting would be enjoyable.

"I hope Papa will take me riding." Jamie peered at him, looking shy, but Lucas was glad his son felt bold enough to express himself. The boy was gradually coming out of the cocoon that he'd been wrapped up in living alone with Heather.

"I imagine that could be arranged, son. But first, finish your breakfast. A man needs a full stomach to work all morning."

Jamie frowned and stared at his porridge. Did he not like the food?

"That's a splendid idea," his mother said. "Heather and I will busy ourselves with redoing Jamie's room and making a list of the supplies we'll need to purchase to finish the project."

Heather sat quietly to his left, sipping her tea. She spoke little during mealtimes, and he wondered if she still felt odd partaking with the family. If he had things his way, he'd keep her close for the rest of their lives.

A quick rap sounded at the back door. Mrs. Overton entered the dining room shortly afterward with Samuel following. The horseman had removed his hat, revealing curly black hair tinged with gray, and he crinkled the brim in his hand. Something had happened.

Lucas stood and crossed the room into the hall, where they could talk and not be overheard. "What is it?"

Samuel followed. He glanced at the family through the doorway then leaned in close and whispered, "We's had us another robbery."

Lucas sighed. "What did they take this time?"

Samuel scratched his ear. "Well now, that be the odd thing. All's they stole was a feed bucket and an ol' horse blanket."

Lucas excused himself and strode to the barn, with Samuel hurrying to keep up. Three thefts in eight days meant the robber was getting comfortable—bolder—and had to be somewhere close by. How long before he decided to break into the house—or until someone got hurt?

In the barn, he surveyed the tack room, looking for anything amiss. "Everything here seems in order. Why would someone risk capture just to steal a bucket and blanket?" It made no sense.

"Just downright foolhardiness if'n you asks me." Samuel shrugged and picked up an embroidered handkerchief. "Found this wheres the blanket was."

The linsey-woolsey fabric had neat but almost childlike stitching around the outer edge. Had the thief accidentally dropped this? Left it as payment for what he took? Lucas shook his head. A wooden pail was easy enough to make if you had the skill, and the blanket wasn't overly expensive, but both were worth far more than a simple handkerchief. Something had to be done to stop the thefts.

He set the handkerchief on a high shelf. "Leave that there,

and don't let anyone else touch it. Send Julius up to the house with horses for him and me. I'll send him to Ben Ellison's house with a note, asking Ben to bring his hunting dogs. Perhaps we can use the cloth to track the thief."

"That's a right good idea. I'll go fetch him."

While Samuel searched for Julius, Lucas hurried back to the house to prepare a note requesting Ben's help. Then he'd ride over to Madison Gardens and see if Richard had encountered the thief or could help in the search.

In his office, he quickly penned the note to Ben, melted some wax over the raw edge of the paper, and stamped the Reed seal into it.

A knock sounded outside his open door, and his mother stood in the hall holding a vase of flowers. She smiled and entered the room. "I brought something to brighten up your work area."

He stood. "This dull place could use something lively."

She set the vase on the back of his desk, and the scent of candle wax faded against the fragrance of the flowers. His mother's silver and blue day dress looked beautiful and blended well with her eyes. "Is something wrong? I couldn't hear your conversation with Samuel, but you both looked worried."

Lucas blew out a heavy breath. "There's been another theft."

His mother laid a hand across her chest. "Oh my. Was anything valuable taken?"

"That's the odd thing. This thief only takes small things, and one or two at a time. A hen, a bucket, a horse blanket. I can't make any sense of it."

"Hmm. . .sounds like things a person might need to survive." Her eyes widened. "You don't suppose it's a runaway slave, do you?"

He laid a hand on her shoulder, hoping to reassure her.

"I sincerely doubt it. I thought that at first, but I can't see a slave staying this long. He'd want to get as far away from his owner as possible."

"Perhaps he feels safe here, knowing that you don't own slaves."

Lucas pursed his lips and shook his head. "I just can't see it. A runaway is still his owner's property and wouldn't be any safer here than somewhere else. As much as I despise slavery, it is legal, and I'd be breaking the law to harbor someone else's slave."

His mother narrowed her eyes and stared at him. "It wouldn't be the first time you've broken the law for a good cause."

He turned and strode to the open doors leading onto the balcony. Across the shaded lawn, he could see Heather and Jamie seated on a quilt in the shelter of a massive live oak in the far corner of the garden. Shrubs in full bloom framed the area in pink, white, and lavender flowers. Such a lovely sight warred with the memories swirling in his mind. "Those days are behind me, Mother. Besides, I was young and headstrong then, determined to free our country from Britain's stronghold. Being a privateer with the blessings of the Patriot government was a way to help the war efforts and to hinder the supply line to the British troops."

His mother crossed the room in a swish of skirts and stood beside him. "You say those days are behind you, yet you refuse to sail your ships except for the trip to Charleston and back. I never understood that."

He clenched his jaw as the memories continued to assail him. "I did things that I'm not proud of. We took lives for the sake of food and ammunition."

"It was war, son. During such dire times, men are often forced to do things beyond what they feel capable of doing."

"That doesn't change the fact of what I did. Sacrificing my

love of sailing on the open sea is my penance to God."

"Lucas, Lucas. You know God has forgiven you. When you became a believer, you repented of your sins, and the blood of Christ washed you clean. You're a new creation. The past has been made pure, and you no longer need to be chained to it."

"I know, Mother, and I believe what you say. But I made an oath to God, and I'll not break it."

She sighed. "I fear one day you will be required to—and then what?"

Lucas shrugged. "I hope that day never comes." He turned to face her. "In the meantime, I'm sending a rider to Ben Ellison's to see if he can come and bring his tracking dogs. I'm off to the Madisons' to recruit Richard's assistance. I mean to catch the thief this day."

"Do invite Caroline to come and stay with us if Richard agrees to help you."

He nodded. "That's a brilliant idea, Mother. Heath—uh. . .Miss Hawthorne and she seemed to get along well in Charleston."

She eyed him with the precision of a hawk high up in the sky watching a poor mouse; then she glanced across the garden to where Heather and Jamie sat. She'd noticed his faux pas, no doubt, and where his gaze had been focused.

He cleared his throat. "I must be off. I want this thief caught before dark. Please see to it that Miss Hawthorne and Jamie stay within sight of the house today."

Without waiting for a response, he strode past his desk, snatched up the letter to Ben Ellison, and stormed from the room. He'd encouraged Heather to keep their budding relationship a secret, but he was afraid he'd just let the cat out of the bag.

eleven

Tired of reading several chapters aloud, Heather closed the book. "What did you think about Robinson Crusoe making friends with Friday?"

Jamie sat on the corner of a blanket shredding a leaf that he'd plucked from a nearby shrub. "I'm glad he didn't have to be alone no more."

" 'Tis *anymore*, Jamie, not *no more*." She smiled. "I am also happy he found a friend." If things went well between her and Lucas, perhaps she wouldn't have to live alone, either. She'd lain awake much of the night, reliving their walk and Lucas's surprising revelation. That he could care for her was almost beyond hope. Had their attraction to each other blossomed because of their common love for Jamie?

Yawning, she noticed Jamie had risen and was creeping toward a bush covered in a blanket of fat white flowers. This garden was an Eden. She couldn't look at the brilliant, flower-covered bushes or breathe in their sweet scent enough. Mrs. Reed had told her that soon the flowers would fade and fall off, and the plants wouldn't bloom again until next spring.

Where would she be then?

A bird suddenly darted out of the bush and flew past Jamie's head. He jumped then glanced at her, grinning. The brown bird with red highlights glided over to a vivid purple shrub and alighted.

"Jamie, if you'll be quiet and watch, there's a fine possibility that you'll see that bird's mate. It will be a bright red."

He lifted his gaze and looked up into the huge tree above them then scanned the garden. The female chirped, and Heather smiled. It almost sounded as if the bird was rapidly repeating, "Here, kitty, kitty, kitty."

Jamie hunkered down and tiptoed toward the female. Heather knew she should scold him for scaring the birds, but the warmth of the day and her lack of sleep made her listless. She understood why many southerners took a rest midday.

She yawned and closed her eyes for a moment, listening to the birdcall and Jamie's soft giggling. If she and Lucas were to marry, Jamie would one day be a big brother to their children. He would like that and be a good one. . . .

Heather felt the sudden sensation of falling into a dark cavern and jerked awake. It took a moment for her to realize she'd been dozing. Stretching, she yawned and looked around. She was outside—not in her bed? Oh yes, she'd been reading to Jamie.

She bolted upright. Where was Jamie? How long had she slept?

Peering up at the sun, she realized that she must have dozed for close to an hour. Panic shot through her like a musket ball. Had Jamie gone inside? Had he wandered off?

"Jamie! Where are you, lad?" She stood and scanned the gardens but didn't see him. "Jamie?"

Her heart throbbing, she picked up the book and quilt and rushed back into the house. Surely he was eating a treat in the kitchen or with his father or grandmother. *Please be there.*

Scolding herself for being so lax, she entered the house and deposited the book and blanket on a bench just inside the back door. She burst into the kitchen.

Mable's startled gaze lifted from her task of slicing a hunk of meat. "Land sakes, you done frightened a dozen years offa me."

"Have you seen Jamie?" Heather franticly searched the kitchen.

"No, miss. Not since breakfast. Did you lose him?"

"I'm sure he must be upstairs. I'll check there." How could she tell the woman that she had indeed lost him? How could she bear it if anything happened to him?

She hurried up the steps then quickly looked in each room, and all but collided with Mrs. Reed as she exited the library, book in hand.

"Oh my dear, what's the big rush?" Mrs. Reed smiled, blue eyes shining.

Heather looked past her, hoping against hope that Jamie was with his grandmother. Tears burned her eyes when she didn't locate him.

Mrs. Reed's smiled faded. "What is it?"

Heather grimaced and broke her gaze. "I was reading to Jamie—and drifted asleep. He was in the garden, watching some birds." She gasped a sob. "Now I can't find him."

Mrs. Reed pulled her into her arms and patted her back. "Now, now, he can't have gone far. We'll gather up the servants and find him quickly." She set her book on a hall table, guided Heather into the parlor, and tugged on a bell pull.

"I feel dreadful." Heather collapsed onto a chair. "Mr. Reed will never trust me with his son again."

"Don't fret so, my dear. I raised two boys and know how they can go wandering off."

Two boys? Lucas had never mentioned a brother. Had he died in childhood? Could he have wandered off like Jamie and never come back? Unshed tears stung her eyes. "Oh, I should never have fallen asleep. I had some things on my mind and didn't rest well last night."

Mrs. Reed stared at her with a knowing look. A tiny smile tugged at the corner of her lips. Had Lucas told his mother about them after requesting her silence?

"Do you suppose Jamie could be with his father?" Heather asked.

Mrs. Reed shook her head. "No, Lucas rode over to the Madisons' a short while ago. I suspect he'll be back soon with them in tow. Let's see if we can't locate Jamie before they return."

Mrs. Overton hurried into the room, the jingling keys on her chatelaine heralding her arrival. "You rang for me, ma'am?"

"Aye, Jamie has gone missing, and we need to find him quickly. Please assemble as many servants as you can to join us in the search."

Mrs. Overton nodded and sped from the room.

"Now, I will thoroughly search the house, and why don't you look farther outside?" She patted Heather's hand. "We will find the boy. The good Lord wouldn't send him this far to us and let something happen to him."

"I wish I had your faith."

"You can, dear. All you must do is repent of your sins and believe that Jesus is the Son of God and that He died for you. Trusting God during difficult times can be quite reassuring."

Heather nodded, wondering if that was why Mrs. Reed seemed so calm in the face of such a calamity. She rose, anxious to continue her search. "I'll check the outbuildings, garden, and"—she swallowed hard—"down by the pond and the river."

"You know how much Jamie loves the horses. Why don't you start with the barn? Then I can have the servants search around the water." Her smiled wobbled, revealing that she wasn't quite as composed as she portrayed.

"Aye, Mrs. Reed."

"Won't you please call me Amelia?"

Heather offered a weak smile and a brief nod and hurried from the room. Why hadn't she thought of the barn? Jamie frequently asked his father to take him to see the horses or to go for a ride. She all but jogged the distance to the stable. When she stepped inside, it took a moment for her eyes to adjust to the dimmer lighting. She lifted a hand to her nose, blocking the odor of horses and hay. Dust motes drifted lazily on the sunlight shining in the open doors and windows. A horse whickered at her, but there was no sign of Jamie.

She stood still, trying to listen in the quiet over the thrumming of her heart. Could he be hiding? If he was and he saw her, she was certain he'd start giggling. When she heard nothing, she called to him, "Jamie, are you here? Please come out."

After a few moments, she hurried to the far side of the barn. Jamie had thoroughly enjoyed the tour of the servants' outbuildings when they'd taken a walk down that way one morning. Perhaps he'd gone to watch the candlemaker who had so fascinated him or to play with some of the servants' younger children that two older women cared for while their parents worked.

Sweat streamed down her spine as she quickened her pace. The servants' village came into view. She received odd looks from the servants when she peeked into the weaving and sewing houses, the candle- and soap makers' cabin, and the dye house. Her hands shook, and she battled tears. Where could he have gone?

Two large black men walked toward her. She recognized one of them as the man who often worked in the barn. She picked up her skirt and hurried toward him. "Please, sir, have you seen Jamie?"

The taller man's dark eyes widened. "That boy, he be missin'?"

"Yes. I can't find him anywhere." Tears coursed down her cheeks, but she cared little. Her life was over if anything happened to Jamie.

"I'm Samuel, and this here be Abraham. We's gonna help you find that boy."

Heather reached out and grabbed the man's calloused hands. "Oh, thank you so much."

"You go gather ever'body and ask if they done seen Master Jamie." Samuel nodded to Abraham, who took off jogging toward the nearest building. He picked up a mallet and whacked a circle of tin hanging from a cord. A loud *bong* filled the air, and men and women poured from the buildings, gathering together.

"Why don't you go back to the big house? We'll find that boy."

"Perhaps he went to play with the other children."

Samuel gently turned her toward the house. "We'll check there. You go keep Miz Reed comp'ny."

Heather nodded and wandered back to the house. Her feet felt as if she were wearing lead shoes. Never in the years she'd cared for Jamie had she ever let him out of her sight until coming to Charleston. What if. . .

All manner of heinous thoughts assaulted her. She lifted her hands to her face and sobbed. "Oh, God, please watch over him. I'll do anything You want if You'll let us find Jamie, safe and sound."

The thud of quickly moving hooves drew near, then stopped. Leather creaked. "Heather, what's the matter? Why are you crying?"

Her tears flowed faster at the sound of Lucas's voice, and she couldn't bear to look at him. "I've lost Jamie."

His arms encircled her. "Shh. . .tell me what happened."

She longed to nuzzle against his chest and stay there, but she couldn't. She didn't deserve to. What would happen to Lucas if he lost his son when he'd barely gotten to know the lad? "I—I was reading to him—and I fell asleep."

"I see. Where have you looked for him?"

At the clipped tone of his voice, she stepped out of his arms, and her cheeks warmed when she realized Richard Madison was also present atop his horse. "Your mother is searching the house. I checked the barn and the servants' work houses. Samuel has gathered the servants, and they are also searching." Heather's chin wobbled, but she stayed her tears.

Lucas lifted his tricorne and ran his hand through his black hair. "Has anyone checked near the river or ponds? You know how Jamie likes searching for tadpoles."

She turned toward the river and noticed a trio of men headed toward the dock. "They're checking now."

"How long has he been missing?"

"I don't know." Heather winced. "Perhaps an hour."

"Go stay with Mother. We will find him."

Lucas mounted, and he and Richard Madison rode at a gallop toward the servants' quarters. Heather forced her feet to move toward the house. In spite of the warm sun beaming down on her, a cold shiver made her cross her arms. If anything happened to Jamie, Lucas would forever blame her.

❧

Lucas shot one prayer after another toward heaven, but a sense of dread still clung to him like barnacles on a ship's hull. How could Heather have been so careless? Where would Jamie go if given his freedom to explore without an adult along? What if the thief had found Jamie and done him harm or held him for ransom?

Lucas rode his horse to the barn and tugged Liberty to a stop just outside the doors. "Samuel!"

Richard followed, his eyes filled with compassion. "I'm sorry about this, Lucas. We'll find him."

Lucas nodded. When his servant didn't answer, he spun his horse around and trotted him alongside the creek. Surely Jamie wouldn't venture near the water after being warned about alligators.

A motion drew Lucas's gaze toward the road leading to the house. A wagon with a saddled horse tied behind it rolled toward him. "Good. Ben Ellison is here."

When he'd sent someone for Ben, he surely never expected he'd have to use the dogs to find Jamie. "Richard, could you ride up to the house and ask Heather for something Jamie has worn recently? We can use it so Ben's dogs can catch his scent."

Richard nodded and rode off, while Lucas trotted Liberty forward to meet Ben. Two brown and white hound dogs jumped up on the back of the wagon's bench seat and bayed a greeting.

"I'm mighty obliged to you for coming so quickly," Lucas said.

"Happy to do it." Ben smiled. His curly gray hair stuck out from under his hat in ringlets. His fuzzy eyebrows and beard were still a dark brown that matched his friendly eyes. Ben was a neighbor who always came if called on. "If you have a thief here, he just might hit my place or my daughter's next. It's best we see to this problem before someone gets hurt."

Lucas clenched his jaw, not quite ready to tell his neighbor about Jamie, but there was nothing to be done about it. He needed Ben's help. While they waited for Richard to return, Lucas explained about Jamie and how he was missing.

Ben scratched his beard. "That's a shame that you just found your boy and now he's gone off somewhere. But my Lolly and Molly will find him." The dogs whimpered and wagged their tails at the sound of their names. Ben jumped down to the ground then motioned for the dogs to do the same. He untied his horse from the back of the wagon and walked toward Lucas.

Richard galloped back with the shirt Jamie had worn yesterday in his hand. He gave it to Ben. The dogs began baying again, as if sensing the chase that was soon to ensue.

"Where was the boy last seen?" Ben asked.

"In the gardens." Lucas pointed toward the house.

"That's where we'll start." Ben mounted, and they rode to the area in the garden where Heather said she had been reading to Jamie. Ben slid off his horse then called his dogs and held the shirt for them to sniff. Tails wagged and the dogs yipped, their eyes riveted on their owner. He waved a hand in the air. "Search, Lolly. Search, Molly."

The dogs ran from tree to shrub to grassy alcove. One of them bayed. The other dog joined in, and both bolted out of the garden toward the barn. They stopped and sniffed around a bush a short distance from the barn then dashed off in the direction of the pond. Ben jumped back on his horse. "They've got the scent!"

All three horses jumped the low hedge and galloped after the dogs, which were already nearing the arched bridge. Lucas's heart throbbed in time with Liberty's hoofbeats. "Please, Father, keep Jamie safe. Watch over him."

twelve

Heather paced in front of the parlor window. The men had followed the howling dogs across the creek and into the trees on the far side. What could have compelled Jamie to venture in that direction? Had he gone to the creek in search of tadpoles? Had he chased a bird so far that he'd gotten lost?

"Heather, please come and sit down." Amelia patted the sofa beside where she sat. "Caroline and I would like to pray together for Jamie."

"It will give us something more constructive to do than worrying." Caroline Madison smiled. "And it's the best way we can help. The Scriptures say, 'For where two or three are gathered together in my name, there am I in the midst of them.'"

Twisting her hands, Heather glanced at the two women. "I prayed earlier—when I was looking for Jamie." She blinked back the tears burning her eyes. "I told God I'd do anything for Him if He saved Jamie."

Amelia rose and came to Heather then took her hand. She gently led her to the sofa and pressed down on her shoulders until she sat. Amelia resumed her seat. "God doesn't bargain for our love and obedience. He loves us freely and longs for us to love Him in return. He will protect Jamie because He loves him far more than we ever could. He loves us so much that He allowed His own precious Son, Jesus, to die for our sins."

Heather had never heard the Bible message explained in such simple terms before. She listened, wondering again how

Amelia could remain so calm in the face of her grandson's disappearance. Her heart longed for that peace—to know God. To have Someone she could talk to when she was alone. Someone to comfort her in troubling times such as this one. "What do I have to do then to become a child of God?"

Amelia's warm smile chased away some of Heather's anxiety. "The Scriptures say to believe on the Lord Jesus Christ and you shall be saved. We are also instructed to repent of our sins."

Heather glanced at Caroline, who smiled and nodded her agreement. "It's that simple."

She stared out the window, longing for peace. Most of her life had been spent in turmoil. Her mother had lost several babies then finally died giving birth to another child who failed to survive. Her father had disappeared for months at a time, leaving her in the care of a coldhearted governess. When he was home, he drank until he could no longer function. Then just when she came of age and hoped she might find a decent man to marry and give her some stability, her father had lost their home by gambling and had hauled her off to the Nova Scotia wilderness. Deborah had been her only close companion until she died, and then a year ago, Heather's father passed away, leaving only Jamie and a few neighbors, none of whom she was close to.

She heaved a heavy sigh. If God could fill the emptiness in her heart, then she welcomed Him. She looked at Amelia and nodded. "How do I ask Him?"

Amelia took hold of her hands. "Just what I said before. Talk to God, either out loud or in your head. Tell Him that you believe that Jesus Christ is His Son and that He died to save you from sin."

Bowing her head, Heather focused her attention on her sins. She hadn't been a naughty child, but surely she'd done many things that were wrong in God's eyes. She couldn't bear to say the words out loud, so she prayed in her mind. *Dear God, I do believe in Jesus, Your Son, and I thank You that He died for me. I'm truly sorry for the bad things I've done, whether intentionally or not. Forgive me for losing Jamie.*

The weight of that thought caught in her throat, making it hard to breathe. But she pressed on, determined to make peace with God. *Thank You for saving me. And please, Lord, show Lucas where Jamie is.*

She sat with her head bowed for a while longer. She wasn't sure, but it felt as if the strain of the day lessened. Finally, she peered up, catching both women eyeing her with open curiosity. "I did it."

A breath whooshed out of Amelia, warming Heather's face. She cupped Heather's cheek. "Wonderful."

Caroline reached out and bridged the gap between them, touching Heather's arm. "I'm so happy for you. The angels in heaven are rejoicing this day."

"I hope the angels are helping look for Jamie." Heather ducked her head and picked a seedpod off her skirt.

Both Amelia and Caroline chuckled. "I'm sure they are," Amelia said. "Now, would you like to join Caroline and me in prayer for Jamie?"

"Aye. I would." Heather closed her eyes, feeling a unity with God she'd never before encountered. Her chest warmed as Amelia pleaded out loud for Jamie's safe return. Heather felt as if God granted her the assurance that the lad would be home soon. One thing was for certain—she was not the same woman she'd been this morning. God had washed her clean—white as snow.

❧

That evening as the sun began to set, Heather lit several lanterns and hung them on the front porch to help Lucas find his way back home. Amelia did the same upstairs and placed them in the windows, while Caroline helped Mable in the kitchen. With the light fading, the men would soon cease their search. Jamie would be frightened and alone all night. "Please, Father. Bring them home. All of them."

Heather opened the door to go inside when she heard a dog bark. She spun around and hurried to the railing, searching the twilight. Large, dark shapes emerged from the trees and plodded toward her. Lucas!

She snatched up a lantern and scurried down the stairs. One horse broke into a gallop and closed the distance. Lucas stared down at her, looking tired and revealing nothing in his expression. But where was Jamie?

Her heart near shattering, she gazed at the silhouettes of the other horses but couldn't make out if he was on one of them. Then she looked up at Lucas again and noticed the little hands on his waist. "Jamie!"

"Aunt Heather!"

Lucas slid Jamie around and lowered him to the ground. Heather nearly dropped the lantern in her effort to grab hold of the lad. "Oh Jamie. You scared half my life off of me."

He hugged her neck so hard she could barely breathe. She squeezed him back, relishing the scent that was only his.

"Ow. That hurts."

Reluctantly, she released him. "Where were you? Why did you run off?"

"I didn't. I was chasing that bird. Then I saw a squirrel and chased it. It went up a tree. So I decided to go in the barn and see the horses."

"You know you're not supposed to go there alone."

He shrugged and glanced up at his father. Lucas dismounted but didn't add anything.

"I didn't. I saw a lad sneak out of the barn carrying the

blanket Samuel puts on Papa's horse. He didn't see me because I hid behind a bush."

Heather clutched her chest. Jamie had encountered the thief?

"I followed to see where he took the blanket. I thought he must be the thief Papa was looking for."

"Oh Jamie, don't you know how dangerous that was? What if that lad had hurt you?"

The dogs scurried over then flopped down in the grass near Jamie, their pink tongues hanging limp from the side of their mouths. They looked well satisfied. The other two horses stopped just past Lucas's, and the men dismounted. Richard walked into the circle of light, carrying a sleeping young lass with matted brown hair and a filthy dress. The poor thing was barefoot. Ben joined them, leading a dirty lad who looked about ten years old. His tattered clothing was a grimy gray. His shoulder-length blond hair was ratted and held pieces of hay, and listless green eyes peered at her. She glanced at Lucas.

"We need to get these children cleaned up so they can eat," he said. "We're all starving."

Quick footsteps sounded in the darkness, and Samuel appeared. "Praise be to God. You's found him."

Lucas nodded. "Yes, thanks to the good Lord's guidance and Ben's dogs." He handed his horse's reins to Samuel. "Could you also see to the other horses?"

"Yassah. Don't you worry. I's a gonna take good care of 'em." He gathered up the reins and led the three horses away.

Jamie tugged her arm. "I haven't eaten since breakfast."

"And whose fault is that?" She was so relieved to have him back that her worry turned to irritation.

"Jamie knows it was wrong to run off after Kit." Lucas rubbed the lad's hair.

"I was just trying to protect our stuff, Papa."

"I know, and I appreciate that, but next time come and find me or one of the other men. Run on along now. Your grandmother will be anxious to see you."

Jamie trotted off toward the big house, but when he reached the stairs, he turned back toward them and waved. Richard and Ben followed along with the two orphans in tow. Heather, not ready to be separated from Jamie again, started to follow, but Lucas grabbed her arm.

"Wait."

She turned to face him. Was he going to discharge her now? Did he despise her for falling asleep and allowing Jamie to wander off? And where did he find those children? "Who is Kit?"

Lucas sighed, his warm breath touching her face. "He's the boy. The girl is Janey, his sister."

Her heart ached for the ragamuffins. "Where did you find them?"

"They'd set up camp about a half mile from here in a group of trees near the creek. I'm surprised the field-workers never saw them since they walk past those trees every day on their way to the rice fields and back."

"But where did they come from?" Heather relaxed now that Lucas wasn't snipping at her as he'd done earlier in the day.

"Charleston. Their father was a sailor who died at sea. Their mother—" Lucas stared up at the sky. "She became a dock strumpet after her husband's death. She couldn't feed her children, so she started taking in men. One of them killed her, and Kit took his sister and ran away, fearing for their lives. Somehow they stowed away on a vessel bound inland. Kit's been stealing things just so they can survive."

"Those poor children." In spite of the lad endangering

Jamie, she couldn't help feeling sympathy for him and his sister.

A horse whinnied off in the distance, and a warm gust of wind caused the lantern to flicker and go out. Heather held her skirts down. One might even call their environment romantic, if there weren't so many unknowns. "So how did you find the children?"

"The dogs led us to Jamie—and he was with them, trying to talk them into returning here with him."

Heather smiled. That was her lad—kind and generous, just like his father. She swallowed hard. Did Lucas still care for her? Losing a man's only son could cause some men to become fighting mad. Lucas seemed overly quiet and hadn't said anything except to answer her questions. "Well. . .I suppose I should get inside and help get the children cleaned up. Whatever will you do with them?"

"They have no family. Richard seems to think Caroline will be agreeable to taking them in. They've wanted children for a long while but haven't had any."

"That would be nice. She would make a wonderful mother." She started to turn away but couldn't. "I'm so sorry, Lucas. I didn't sleep well last night—I know it's not a decent excuse. I fell asleep when I should have been watching Jamie." Her lower lip trembled. "I don't know how I would have survived if something had happened to him."

"I know. I felt the same." He exhaled another sigh. "I'm sorry I was so short with you. When you said Jamie was missing, I didn't. . .know how to bear it. I'll admit I was upset with you, but I was wrong." He stepped closer and found her hands in the dark. "I was a young boy once, and I know how often I tried to sneak away from my governess. Will you forgive me?"

Heather closed her eyes, not believing what she was

hearing. He wasn't going to turn her out. He wanted *her* to forgive *him*. "I'm the one who needs *your* forgiveness."

"Then shall we agree to forgive one another?" His voice took on a husky tone.

"Aye," she whispered. "I. . .um. . .asked God to save me today and prayed with your mother and Caroline for you to find Jamie."

He ran his hand down the side of her head. "I can't tell you how happy that makes me. My relationship with God is the only thing I place above family."

She longed to be a part of that family but was afraid to hope. Too many things in her life hadn't gone as planned. "You're a good man, Lucas."

"Would you run screaming to the house if I were to kiss you?"

Heather giggled at the silly picture that popped into her mind. "Nay, I would not."

He drew his hand to her face. Her breath quickened.

"I don't know how I survived all these years without Jamie and you in my life. Do you understand, Heather? I fear I am falling in love with you."

Tears stung her eyes for the hundredth time that day. "I feared you'd release me."

"Never." He cleared his throat. "I mean, only if you wish to be released."

She shook her head. He lowered his face, and his lips met hers. She clutched his arms tightly; then he drew her to him, deepening the kiss. It was everything she'd dreamed of and more, but it was over far too soon.

He pressed his forehead against hers. "Is our relationship advancing too quickly for you? I'll be thirty in a few weeks, and I'm ready to move on with my life. Deborah will always hold a place in my heart, but that's in the past. I want you to be my future."

Heather leaned her head against his chest and wrapped her arms around his waist. He smelled manly—of the outdoors. "I care for you, too, Lucas. I've never been close to a man before."

He leaned back as if to look in her face. The lights from the house faintly illuminated his surprised expression. Then he grinned. "You mean I'm the only man you've ever kissed?"

"You don't have to say it as if you're so proud. I had Jamie to care for and never found a man that interested me."

His grin widened. "Until now."

"Aye."

He cupped his hands around her face. "Good. I like that." He kissed her again, their lips and their breath melding together. After he placed another quick peck on her lips, he stepped back. "I suppose we should go in. Mother will call out the militia if we don't return soon."

"I imagine she would." Heather took his arm.

Lucas bent and retrieved the lantern then escorted her to the house. Excitement pulsed through her.

Jamie was safe.

God had redeemed her, and she was falling in love.

This miserable day had turned out surprisingly well.

thirteen

After depositing Jamie into Samuel's care, Heather hurried back to the house. While he was occupied with his riding lesson, she was determined to share her idea with Lucas. She'd hoped to have a surprise party, but with Lucas's birthday just two weeks away, she'd need his help and his mother's to pull off such a large event.

Hurrying up the steep stairs to the back door, she considered how much had changed since she'd first come to Charleston. Jamie and his father were getting along as if Lucas had raised him from birth. Such a feat could only be the hand of God.

Her heart warmed at thoughts of her heavenly Father and how He'd come into her heart so recently. Her whole outlook on life had changed. She now had hope, where before she had only an abysmal future. Her relationship with Lucas had continued to grow, and she might soon find herself married. A smile tugged at her lips at the thought of being Lucas Reed's wife. And too, she'd never have to leave Jamie. He'd be her son, just as she'd dreamed. Afraid to allow her hopes to soar too high, she pulled them back. From now on, she would leave her future to God.

She searched the downstairs rooms then headed upstairs when she didn't find Lucas. He was probably in his office, as he was most early afternoons. Her footsteps echoed through the open upstairs parlor where guests were generally entertained. She could hold the party here, but Amelia thought it best to have it at the Charleston home so the majority of the guests would have less of a distance to travel.

Lucas wasn't in his office, but rather leaning against a pillar on the veranda reading a book. She smiled at the picture he made. Tall, handsome, engaged in a mental activity instead of the physical ones in which he so often participated—the ones that had shaped his well-formed muscles and broad shoulders. She wondered at how she had ever despised this man. But she hadn't truly known him then.

The warm breeze ruffled her skirts, drawing Lucas's gaze from his book. The smile he sent her stirred her senses and made her want to rush into his arms. Instead, she forced her feet to take small, feminine steps. Lucas straightened and tucked the book under his arm.

"To what do I owe the pleasure of this unexpected meeting?"

Heather giggled. "You just saw me at luncheon, less than an hour ago."

He placed a hand over his heart. "But it seems as if years have passed."

"You goose."

He faked a wince. "Oh, the lady maligns me when, in fact, my heart doth take wing whene'er I see her. If that makes me a goose, then yes, I am one." He bowed and pretended to tip a hat, which he wasn't wearing. "Goose Reed at your service, miss."

Laughing, Heather shook her head and stared out at the beautiful river scene. Spanish moss hung from the trees, dancing in the breeze like fine lace on a lady's gown. Moss covered the top of the water, making it a bright green. Though just midspring, countless flowers bloomed in the cultured garden.

Lucas moved beside her, his shoulder touching hers. "It's a lovely sight, is it not?"

"Aye." She nodded.

He turned to face her and lifted his hand to her cheek.

His eyes glowed with love—for her. She still had a hard time grasping that thought, with her coming from a Loyalist family and his being American patriots.

"All of this pales in comparison to you."

Her breath caught in her throat.

He smiled, making her stomach feel as if butterflies were doing a winged battle in it. "I thought my chance for love had passed me by, but then you and Jamie came into my life. How did I ever live without you?"

Heather hated the doubt that crept in and spoiled the moment, but she still couldn't help wondering if his love for her was tied to Jamie. He'd have never met her if not for the boy, yet she wanted him to love her for who she was, not because she brought his son to him. Until she knew for sure, she couldn't allow him to kiss her again. She wouldn't share her affections with any man but the one meant to be her husband. She forced herself to face the garden again. "I can see why you prefer to stay here instead of in Charleston."

He scowled. "You don't like our Charleston home?"

"What?" Her gaze darted to his. Had she offended him? "Aye, I do, but I so love the serenity here, and you don't see your closest neighbors when you're on your porch."

He chuckled. "There is that, though I do miss the ocean when I'm here."

"Your mother said you used to sail frequently but that you no longer do. Can I ask why not?"

His jaw tightened, and all merriment fled. He remained silent so long that she thought he might not answer. "It's not something I often talk about, but you'll find out sooner or later if you remain here for long. I'd just as soon you heard the truth from me."

Heather turned to face him, concerned with the serious tone in his voice. Perhaps she shouldn't have asked, but she longed to know everything about the man she was quickly growing to love.

He pursed his lips and drew in a deep breath. "I do fear, though, that the fondness you've developed for me will flee when you learn the truth."

"I sincerely doubt that. A relationship that's worth its salt must be built on truth and not secrets."

"You're right." He gestured to a chair behind her. "Would you care to sit?"

Heather shook her head. "I'm fine. Thank you."

"I suppose I should start telling you about Marcus."

"Who is Marcus?"

❧

Lucas loathed mentioning his brother's name. He couldn't tell Heather the whole truth—that Marcus was really Jamie's father—but she deserved to know most of the story. He faced her again, seeing the curiosity gleaming in her lovely eyes. "Marcus is my brother. My twin brother."

Her mouth formed an O, but she remained silent.

"He was born just a few minutes after me, but you know the traditions of England and of the father passing down his holdings to his eldest son. We may have lived in America, and my father's family in Barbados, but Father was still English, through and through.

"As a boy, Marcus was happy and content with our mother's love and attention, but as we grew older, he became aware of how our father favored me." Lucas clenched his jaw. He'd have gladly shared the family wealth with his brother, but his father wouldn't hear of it. "When Marcus realized that he could never compete for our father's love or his blessing, he began rebelling. He started drinking at a young age and causing all sorts of trouble. Mother tried to keep him reined in, but her love wasn't enough anymore."

Heather laid her hand on his arm. "I'm sorry, Lucas. I understand. My father didn't have a son, and if he had retained his wealth, it would have gone to my cousin rather than to me."

He nodded, glad she understood the situation at least partially. He took her hand and continued. "Marcus and I had a falling out, and then he left. I haven't seen him in nearly a decade." Close to eight years, he wanted to tell her, but then she might piece things together.

"It must be difficult being separated from your only sibling. I have none, so I can't imagine what that feels like."

"It does bother me, but Marcus caused so much trouble I actually felt relieved that he was gone." But fiercely angered that he took Deborah with him.

"Thank you for telling me. Your mother mentioned having two sons, but I never asked her about that."

He appreciated that his mother left the decision up to him as to how much to tell Heather about Marcus. As much as he'd like to end the conversation about his past, he had to tell Heather about his time in the navy, and he dreaded doing so for fear she'd no longer want to have anything to do with him.

"Nothing you've said so far could change how I feel for you. Did you think my affections were so shallow?"

Lucas gritted his teeth, wishing he didn't have to continue. "You've not heard all. During the Revolution, I served the colonies as a privateer. I would sometimes raid British ships and steal their cargo."

Heather's eyes went wide, and her struggle was evident.

Please, heavenly Father, don't let me lose her over this.

"A British seventy-four-gun man-of-war could hurl tons of hot iron with a few of her broadsides, but she wasn't much use when she ran aground. I captained a sleek Chesapeake

Bay schooner, armed with a handful of six-pounder cannons. We'd run the blockade, easily outsailing Britain's larger ships, and slip away to the West Indies to trade tobacco for gunpowder and cash or credit to support the Revolution."

Heather's hands gripped the porch railing, but she didn't comment.

"We were fighting for our freedom."

"Was it so terrible being a British colony?"

"We were heavily taxed but had no say in how things were run here. We were under the authority of a ruler who lived across the ocean, one who cared little about what happened here, save to extract burdensome taxes from us." He turned her to face him. "We've set up our own government and laws that will benefit the people of this great land. We're free now. Do you know how that feels?"

She shook her head. "I don't suppose I do."

"What I did still haunts me, even though the deeds were done under the guise of war. After I became a Christian, I gave up sailing, though I love it. I build ships, but I haven't sailed on the open seas since the war ended." He heaved a sigh, glad to have told her about his past. It would be up to her whether she found it within herself to forgive him for the deeds perpetrated against her countrymen or if she left at first light.

❧

Heather's heart ached from the heavy burden that Lucas had heaped on her. She ought to be livid that he'd fought against Britain and possibly her own father, but that was all in the past. What bothered her most was how his own heart must hurt over his estrangement from his brother.

"So, do you hate me now?" Lucas asked.

"Nay, even though a part of me says I should."

His tight expression relaxed, and he blew out a breath.

"But there's something I don't understand. You told me that God loves us and forgives past sins once we've confessed them, and I believe that now, so why do you feel you have to give penance by giving up sailing?"

He shrugged. "I just do. It's difficult for someone else to understand."

She shook her head and ran her hand down his arm. "I think you're wrong, Lucas. If you're forgiven, God wouldn't expect you to endure penance. The blood of Christ has set us free."

His brows dipped down. "You don't understand. It's not just the war; it's Marcus, too. I should have done more to keep him here." He waved his hand in the air. "I didn't ask for all of this. I'd have gladly shared it with him. I just had to wait until after my father died, because he was so set against it. Once the estate and business became mine, I was free to do with them as I wished. But Marcus couldn't wait. He wanted things when he wanted them. Even—"

She gazed up at him. "Even what?"

He turned his back to her. "Nothing. I was afraid explaining all this would drive you away. I don't expect you to understand." He walked inside then spun back around. "And please forget this nonsense about having a party for me. It isn't necessary."

She opened her mouth to call to him as he strode away, but she remained quiet instead. If anything, she was the one who should be upset. Imagine kindhearted, generous Lucas a privateer. A warrior fighting for his freedom against an overwhelmingly strong opponent. Nobody expected the colonists to win the war, but they had by their grit and determination.

Had God been on *their* side all along?

fourteen

Heather stared at her list of things to do before the night of Lucas's birthday party and heaved a sigh. How would she accomplish it all?

Footsteps drew her away from her task. Amelia glided into the room, her face glowing from her afternoon rest. "How are things progressing, my dear?"

"I fear I may have overestimated my abilities."

"Pshaw." Amelia waved her hand in the air. "It's a simple thing to organize a gathering. Make a list of food, and I'll see to it that Miss Haversham, our housekeeper in Charleston, gets it. She will arrange everything."

"It doesn't seem fair to ask her to take on such a big event."

"Nonsense. It's part of her duties. The Reeds have entertained far too little. Lucas has no desire to plan such events, and I confess that my heart hasn't been in it either."

"Am I wrong to want to do this?" Heather leaned her cheek against her hand.

Amelia rested her palm on Heather's arm. "No dear. It's a fine thing you want to do and will be good for Lucas. Besides, it will be the perfect time to make an announcement about Jamie."

Heather smiled. "I want to thank you and Lucas for so willingly accepting Jamie into your family. I know it can't have been easy for either of you,"

Amelia glanced around the parlor. "Where is my grandson?"

"Lucas took him riding. They're on a quest to find an alligator."

Amelia chuckled. "Boys will be boys." She sobered and gazed into Heather's eyes. "I should be thanking *you* for bringing Jamie to us. That boy has given me new life. I'd given up hope on Lucas marrying and becoming a father. Jamie is a wonderful boy."

"I think of all the wasted time I put in worrying about bringing him to you. I wish I could have done it sooner. I wish Deborah would have had the nerve to face Lucas once she learned she was with child."

Amelia pursed her lips and looked away. "Lucas loved her so much. He would have welcomed her return. But life for her would have been difficult with people knowing she'd borne a child out of wedlock. I can understand why she chose to stay away."

"What of her parents? I don't believe she ever told them of Jamie."

"I don't know. All I heard was that they returned to England after spending much of their wealth and several years searching for her."

" 'Tis sad they couldn't have enjoyed Jamie while he was so young."

Amelia tapped the table. "Perhaps I should write to them. They should know they have a grandson."

Heather straightened, doubt niggling at her. "But what if they decide to seek custody?"

"Hmm. . .I can see where that could be an issue. Perhaps Lucas should have some kind of legal document proving Jamie is his son. I do believe the law holds that a child first belongs to his father."

"Aye. 'Tis a wise idea. I can testify that Deborah admitted Lucas is Jamie's father. And Lucas has that letter from her. That could be entered in as evidence."

"I'm not sure that would be helpful." Amelia rose suddenly

and tugged on a long narrow tapestry that rang a bell in the kitchen. "Some tea would taste good right about now."

"Aye, it would." She glanced down at her list of party guests. "Will the Charleston house be too crowded if we invite twenty people?"

"No, I don't think so. Besides the dining room and the great room, we can use the piazza. We should be able to easily handle that number."

"Here's the list of names you gave me. Is there anyone we should add before we issue the invitations?"

Amelia quickly read down the page. The maid walked up to the table and waited. "I suppose there are always others to invite, but I don't want Lucas to feel overwhelmed. He's not one for crowds." She looked up. "Oh Talia, would you please bring tea and biscuits for Miss Hawthorne and me?"

"Aye, ma'am." The maid scurried from the room, her feet tapping across the wooden floor.

"Lucas asked me to cease plans for the party," Heather said. "Do you think we should?"

Amelia shook her head. "No, it will be good for him. You're good for him."

Heather's cheeks warmed. She flashed an embarrassed smile and looked away. "I'm not so sure of that."

Lucas's mother leaned forward, resting her arms on the table. "I am. For so long, Lucas has been caught up in his work. He not only oversees the shipbuilding enterprise, but it's nothing for him to actually get out there and work on a ship himself. Many of our stature looked down on him for doing such menial labor."

"But you don't?" Heather could easily see Lucas hanging from a rope, sanding wood or hammering the side of a vessel.

"No, I think it's admirable that he wants to experience every facet of the business. I believe it helps him to better understand the complete workings."

"You're an unusual woman, Amelia."

She cocked her head and smiled. "Thank you, dear. We have too many close-minded people in Charleston. God would have us look at things from different vantage points. Take slavery, for instance. It's an abysmal, degrading venture." She shook her head and pressed her lips together. "I've heard of planters who have broken up slave families. Separated husbands from wives, children from parents. I fear God will punish us one day for mistreating His people so."

" 'Tis refreshing to hear someone from the South speak in such a manner. How do your neighbors tolerate your attitude?"

Amelia rose and walked to the open double doors and stared out at the garden. "We have enemies, certainly, but there are others who believe as we do yet simply can't afford to free their slaves and in turn pay them a wage."

Heather stood and crossed the room to stand beside Amelia. "Well, I for one admire you for not keeping slaves." She shivered as a thought raced across her mind. If she left and returned to Canada, she would know just what it was like to be separated from the child she loved.

"I know of a nice string quartet we could hire to play for the party. Would you like that?"

Heather nodded. "Aye, but I do feel odd that the party was my suggestion and you're having to pay for it all."

Amelia wrapped an arm around Heather. "Lucas is my son. I should have been the one to think of the party, and I thank you for your suggestion. It's a grand idea. If only. . ."

"Are you thinking of Marcus?"

Amelia's eyes widened. "You know of him?"

"Lucas told me yesterday. I can't imagine how much it must hurt you to never see him."

She shrugged and faced the garden. "Let's walk while we're waiting for the tea."

Amelia took Heather's arm and led her outside and downstairs. The fragrant scent of roses and a myriad of other colorful flowers filled her senses. Yellow butterflies flitted from flower to flower, sampling the sweet nectar. Wisteria clung to a wooden archway, its flowers looking like fresh grapes ripe for the picking. What must it be like to enjoy such beauty almost year-round? The South was growing on her, although she could well do without the heat.

"Marcus was always a morose child who grew into a cranky, discontented young man. Lucas, on the other hand, was a pleasant boy, obedient and eager to please. I tried to give Marcus what he needed. From the time they were born, Cedric lavished praise on Lucas and all but ignored his other son. Dreadful shame, it was. Marcus's jealousy grew until it couldn't be contained."

Heather patted Amelia's arm. "How difficult that must have been for all of you."

"If only Cedric had loved Marcus as he did Lucas, I believe things would have turned out all right. I think Lucas has been hurt the most by all of this. His heart is tender, even now, and it crushed him when Marcus left and—"

Heather had the distinct feeling that Amelia had just censured what she was about to say, but she shrugged off the thought. Of course there were things Amelia couldn't tell her.

"I wish he'd return to us, but sad to say, I don't believe I shall ever see him again." She leaned in close. "There's talk that he's a pirate. It grieves me so to think such a thing of my own son."

Heather shook her head, amazed that twin brothers could turn out so different. If Marcus was truly as wicked as Lucas was good, she hoped their paths never crossed.

❧

Heather opened the door of Jamie's bedchamber and peered down the hallway at the growing crowd in the second-floor great room. Soft music drifted toward her, along with the chatter of voices. She should go back, but she felt so out of place among Lucas's friends and associates.

"When do I get to go to the party?"

Heather closed the door and smiled at Jamie. "Soon. When your father is ready." She stooped down, her blue taffeta silk skirts rustling, and smoothed Jamie's collar. He looked striking with his dark hair and vivid blue eyes in his new, white cotton suit, though the ruffled collar and cuffs were a bit too fancy for a lad, in her opinion. "You look mighty handsome."

"Will I get to eat?"

She blew out a breath. "You can't fool me. I know that you've already eaten."

He leaned against her. "Please, can't I have at least one sweet?"

"We shall see. It's close to your bedtime." She smoothed down his hair where it stood on end. "Do you understand the importance of tonight?"

He nodded.

"Tonight your father is announcing to his close friends that he has a son."

"Why don't they already know that?"

"They may." And she was sure they did and were filled with questions about where said lad had come from. "You are to smile but not talk. Do you understand?"

Jamie nodded again. "These shoes hurt my feet."

"Well, you shan't be wearing them all that long. Try to act like a gentleman. And if anyone asks about your mother, please don't say anything. Especially don't tell them her name."

"Why not?" Innocent blue eyes stared up at her.

How did she explain that Lucas wanted to protect Deborah? To not sully her family name? "Because your father wishes it to remain a secret."

Jamie's brow wrinkled, and he stared up at the ceiling as if thinking deeply. "What did my mother look like?"

"Oh dear lad." She pulled him against her skirts, just as a knock sounded at the door. He was only two when his mother died. How could he remember what Deborah looked like when her image was fading even from Heather's mind? "We should talk more about her, but not tonight." She pulled open the door and revealed the footman.

"Mr. Reed is ready for you and the boy, miss."

"Thank you. We shall be there directly." She shut the door and turned back to Jamie. "Are you ready?"

He nodded and hurried to her side, taking her hand.

"Mind your manners. This is a very important evening for your father and your grandmother. You don't want to embarrass them."

"Aye, mum."

Heather's heart pounded as she made her way down the hall. What would Lucas's guests think of his son? Would they reject him? Cast crude comments his way? Eye him with disdain? *Please, Lord, no.*

fifteen

Lucas's gaze shifted toward Heather the moment she entered the room. The footman rang a bell for attention, and when the room quieted, he announced, "Miss Heather Hawthorne and Master Jamie."

Whispers resounded in speculation as Lucas strode forward to meet his son and the woman who'd stolen his heart. His mother joined them, coming from the other side of the room. Heather looked enchanting in her pale blue gown and with her hair curled, and Jamie looked like a miniature of Lucas. No one would doubt their relationship, though he was sure they'd question where the boy had been the past five years.

He reached down and lifted Jamie into his arms. It wouldn't be too many more years and the boy would be too old to carry on occasion. If only Heather had brought him to Charleston sooner. But tonight was not for regrets. He patted his son's back and turned to the crowd.

"Honored guests, I thank you for coming to celebrate my birthday this night. I, more than anyone, have cause to celebrate, and not because I've reached the ripe old age of thirty."

Chuckles filled the room.

"Aye, you're nigh on ancient." Richard Madison grinned. "Before long, you'll be losing your teeth and finding gray hairs."

Lucas smiled at his friend's jesting. "Better gray hair than none."

The room filled with laughter.

Lucas cleared his throat. "I suppose you're wondering about this fine boy, here." He glanced at Heather, and her smile gave him the courage to continue. Some of the people in this room may choose to no longer associate with him once they knew about Jamie. "A few weeks ago, Miss Hawthorne appeared on my doorstep with young Jamie in tow. I didn't want to listen when she claimed he was my son—"

A unified gasp circled the room.

Lucas held up his hand. "But a letter she had in her possession confirmed that Jamie is a Reed. I've had formal papers drawn up to make everything official, and I now present to you, Master James Reed."

The Madisons led the applause and cheers. Jamie smiled and studied the crowd, but Lucas's stomach churned. He'd been careful not to lie to his friends about Jamie, but how would he respond when people asked about his son's mother?

"Can I have a sweet now?" Jamie asked.

Lucas smiled and glanced at Heather. She lifted one shoulder as if to say it was his decision.

"We've already finished dining," his mother said, "but perhaps the maid could take you to the kitchen for a treat. I imagine there's still some pumpkin pudding left."

Jamie licked his lips and turned to Heather. "May I go now?"

"Do you not wish for him to stay a few moments?" Heather asked.

Lucas shook his head. "I wanted to introduce him tonight, but a fine party is no place for a child to linger, even one as well behaved as Jamie."

"Then I'll take him down for his treat and put him to bed afterward."

"You should stay," Lucas's mother insisted. "Talia can tend to Jamie."

Lucas knew his mother was trying to keep Heather here so people would associate them as a couple. Too bad they couldn't have made an announcement of their own tonight. He never thought it possible he'd desire to marry again, but he longed to make Heather his wife.

She took Jamie from him. " 'Tis no problem. Jamie will go to sleep easier if I see to him."

"Be sure you return. You promised me a dance tonight."

Heather's cheeks turned crimson. Her wide eyes gleamed, and she tipped her head in the slightest of nods. He watched her scurry away with his son, his heart swelling with pride for both of them.

A hand clamped hard on his shoulder, drawing his attention back to his guests.

"I say, you sure surprised us, old man." Ferrill Whitmore's keen gaze bore into him. "How is it you managed to father a child and didn't know about it until now?"

"Simple. The boy's mother chose to keep him a secret."

"Then why send him to you after all these years?" Whitmore twisted the end of his moustache as other guests crowded around, also eager to know more about Jamie, if their curious expressions were any indication.

"She died and left instructions for Miss Hawthorne to bring Jamie to me."

"Sorry for your loss. I mean, I suppose it's that."

"A good woman died, Ferrill. It is a loss."

"Humph! She couldn't have been too good or she wouldn't have—"

Lucas closed the few feet between him and Mr. Whitmore. "Say no more, sir. You're talking about the mother of my son. I'll admit the situation is less than ideal, but I'll not have you slandering Jamie's mother."

Ferrill's left eye twitched, and his warm breath touched

Lucas's face. Finally, the man nodded.

Lucas lifted his chin and faced his guests. "What happened in the past matters not. Jamie is my son. He is an innocent child, and I hope that you will all treat him with the courtesy that befits my station in this community."

Heads nodded, and he caught his mother's proud gaze. His heart warmed at her affirmation. Releasing a pent-up breath, he realized things had gone better than he'd expected. Yes, his life was close to perfect now that Jamie and Heather had entered it. Nothing could change that.

The music started again, and one by one, couples began dancing. Lucas waited for more questions, but none came. He thought about Heather returning and dancing with him.

"You've a right to be smiling, son. That went better than I expected." His mother hugged his arm.

"I'll admit it's a relief that people know about Jamie."

"Well, well, you have a party and don't even invite your own brother."

His mother gasped and spun around. "Marcus!"

Heart racing, Lucas glanced up at the sound of his brother's voice. Had Marcus heard the announcement? Had he overheard the talk about Jamie's mother?

Above all things, Marcus could never know that he'd fathered a son.

His mother hurried to her estranged son. "Welcome home, Marcus."

His twin stared down at their mother, and his hard expression softened for a moment. "Mother, 'tis good to see you're still alive and well."

Tears ran down her cheeks. "My heart has ached for you. Have you returned to us for good?"

Marcus shook his head, sending his long, untamed hair flying over his shoulders. "Nay. I know not why I've returned, but I can see life has continued without me."

Lucas glanced around the room. His friends hovered along the walls, whispering and staring. Women dressed in their colorful gowns huddled near their husbands; some looked worried, others curious. Someone uttered the word *pirate*.

Catching Richard's concerned gaze, he nudged his head toward the door, and his friend nodded. Lucas wanted these people out of here in case his brother came with the intent of causing trouble.

"Mother, if you'll please see to our guests, I'll talk with Marcus."

"But so much time has passed since I last saw him." She cast a longing gaze at her younger son. "Please don't leave. I so want to sit and talk with you. Where have you been all these years?"

Marcus winced. Doffing his tricorne, he bowed, as if to cover up his discomfort. Lucas watched him, his gaze sharp and senses on alert. So the rogue still had a soft spot for their mother. Perhaps all was not lost if the man wasn't completely hardened. But with the many crimes his brother had purportedly committed against ships in the Caribbean, it was foolish to think he could ever live a normal life.

" 'Twas good to see you again, Mother. It warms my heart to know you are well. But I shan't tarry. 'Tis time I was taking my leave."

"But you only just arrived." She clutched her hands to her bosom, a mother aching for a lost child. Seeing Marcus again would only cause her more pain.

"Mother, see to our guests, *please*," Lucas said. She cast another emotion-filled glance at Marcus then turned and glided from the room, her guests following.

Lucas faced his brother. "So, why have you come now?"

Marcus's lips tilted in a cocky smirk, but his hand rested on the hilt of his sword. "I've come to wish you happy birthday, brother."

Lucas sincerely doubted that was the truth, but he chose to be cordial even though all his senses warned him to be on guard. "How have you been?"

Surprise entered Marcus's hard, blue eyes before he schooled his expression. "The life of a pirate is always daring. Looting, plundering, and the like. I've amassed quite a fortune, brother. Perhaps I'm ready to settle down and start a family like you have."

Lucas winced. So he knew about Heather and Jamie.

Marcus's face twisted into a vile grin. "Quite a lovely wench you've wedded and bedded."

"We're not talking about her." He had to steer the conversation in another direction before his brother deciphered the truth. "It's never too late to change, Marcus. Give your heart to God and seek His forgiveness."

His brother snorted, strode across the room, and swigged down a glass of punch. He grimaced and wiped his sleeve across his arm. "What, no ale?"

"I no longer drink spirits."

"You've gone soft, brother. That's what a woman will do to you."

Lucas stepped through the door Marcus opened. "Tell me what happened to Deborah. What did you do to *her*? Is she still alive?" He knew the truth, but it was good that his brother didn't know that.

"I see how much you loved her. How old is your son? Five? Six? Did you wait a whole month before finding another skirt to warm your bed?"

Lucas strode forward, his fist clenching and unclenching. "I searched for Deborah nigh on two years. I loved her with all my heart, but you stole her from me."

Marcus heaved a laugh. "Brother, brother, the wench loved me, not you."

Lucas lifted his chin. "I'm the one she was going to marry."

All manner of emotions crossed his brother's tanned face, but his eyes smoldered like blue fire. "Aye, well, 'tis all in the past now, is it not?"

In Lucas's mind, Deborah's abduction had happened only days ago. "What did you do with her?"

His brother shrugged and took on a bored look. "I grew tired of her sniffling and begging to return to you. I let her off ship along the coast of Canada, where she said she had relatives."

"Why did you not bring her back here?"

"She did not wish to return."

And Lucas knew why. Even though she'd been the victim of a kidnapping, people would still look down on her for spending years aboard a pirate ship and birthing the captain's illegitimate son.

"Do you have any idea how much her parents suffered? She was their only child."

Marcus lifted his hand and glanced at his dirty fingernails. "My goal was to hurt you, not them."

"You succeeded."

Marcus studied him and then grinned. "Good."

Lucas had to try to find a way to reach his brother. He might not get another chance. "Why do you hate me so? It's not my fault I was born first."

"Nay, but you *were* and thus received all our father had to give. His wealth, his admiration, even his love—at least what love he was capable of giving."

Lucas walked over to his brother. "And I'd have shared it all with you."

Marcus snorted a laugh. "I can't imagine why. I would not

have assigned even the smallest parcel to you, had it been within my power."

"I'm not you, brother. Family means more to me than wealth."

"Ha! Easy for a man to say who has more wealth than he knows what to do with. Try livin' in poverty on the streets and see if you feel the same."

"I'm sorry, Marcus. I never wanted this."

His brother's gaze hardened. "And therein lies the rub. You never wanted our father's wealth, but you received it, while I ached for it but got nothing."

"I'm sorry."

"Keep your apologies. I don't want them. 'Twas a mistake to return here." Marcus turned on his heel and strode toward the stairs, boots clicking on the tile and loose shirt fluttering, looking every bit the heinous pirate he was. Lucas surmised he should be thankful that he'd survived the confrontation unscathed. He shook his head. "Lord, turn my brother's heart. Help him to find You and gain freedom from his sin and misery."

He wanted nothing more than to hold Heather and Jamie close. But he still had guests, and protocol dictated that he see to them first. Quitting the room, he heard the buzz of conversation and hurried downstairs. It looked as if most of the guests had fled for the safety of their homes. He cringed, knowing the Reeds would be the talk of the town as one guest after another gossiped about how his pirate brother had disrupted his party. He jogged down the last of the stairs, glad he was in time to bid farewell to the Madisons.

Richard followed his progress down with a worried gaze. "So, you're still alive."

Lucas grinned. "For the time being."

"What did he want—if I might be so bold as to ask?"

Lucas shrugged and put an arm around his mother, drawing her close. He noticed the tears gleaming in her eyes, but she'd held them back for the sake of her guests. She leaned her head against his chest and sniffled.

"Would you like me to have your housekeeper fix you some tea?" Caroline offered.

His mother shook her head. "Thank you, but I'm feeling quite tired and plan to retire soon."

Lucas gently squeezed his mother's shoulders. It would have been better for her if Marcus had never come. He'd only upset their mother, and now she'd most likely spiral off in an emotional ride of "if only she'd done more" or "if only she'd stood up to their father for the way he ignored Marcus." Lucas sighed, hating that she'd question herself. She'd been a kind, loving mother to both of them and didn't deserve Marcus's scorn.

Richard's brows drew together, and the look he gave Lucas set him on edge. "This is probably ridiculous, but I just had a thought. You don't suppose your brother saw you and Heather together around town or heard that you were growing fond of her? What if—"

Richard's eyes grew wide, and Lucas deciphered his thoughts.

Heather.

A pain like the blade of a hard-thrust sword ramming into his heart gripped Lucas. What if Marcus had learned that he had fallen in love again? What if his brother had come to steal Heather away as he had Deborah?

"No! Not again." He quickly set his mother aside and took the stairs three at a time. He couldn't lose Heather before he'd even told her of the depth of his love.

❧

"I like that pun'kin pudding. Could I have some more

tomorrow?" Jamie licked his lips as Heather tugged off his shoes.

"We shall see. Perhaps if there is some leftover. It was tasty with the cinnamon sprinkled on top."

"I liked how it squished between my teeth."

Heather smiled, took Jamie's nightshirt from the wardrobe, and shook it open. A movement near the balcony caught her attention, and she saw Lucas leaning against the doorway, staring at her. He must have come across the piazza to bid Jamie goodnight. Her heart taking wing, she started toward him, but the coldness in his gaze stopped her. Why would he have such animosity for her all of a sudden? Had she done something wrong downstairs?

"Who's that?" Jamie asked as he leaned against her.

"Why, 'tis your father, silly lad."

"Uh-unh. That's not Papa."

Heather looked at the man again, and he pushed away from the door and sauntered out of the shadows toward her. In the light of the room, she realized Jamie was right. This man had a ruffian's look. His hair was longer and his beard unshaven. He wore his linen shirt loose and stained. His short pants stopped just below the knee, as sailors often wore. Where Lucas's eyes burned with intelligence and excitement, this man's smoldered like dark coals. Aye, they were twins, identical in many ways, but so different. Where Lucas emanated kindness and good, this man stank of evil. How could two brothers be so different?

"You've a bright son there." The man pulled his wide-brimmed hat off his head and bowed. "Allow me to introduce meself. I'm Marcus Reed, better known as the Black Mark."

Heather's heart jolted. Here she was alone with a vile pirate and no weapon with which to protect Jamie. She tucked him behind her. "What do you want? You've no business here."

Standing with his hands loosely on his hips, he grinned. "Ah, but you're wrong there. 'Tis me birthday, and I've come for the celebration."

"The party is not in this room, sir. I'm just putting the lad to bed."

"Aye, but what interests me *is* up here. So my brother has a son." The man cocked his head as he stared past her. "The boy has the look of a Reed, does he not?"

Heather's mind raced. What should she do? Should she scream for help? Was the man merely curious and wanting to see his nephew? His sinister tone set her nerves on edge.

"Come hither, boy. Let your uncle have a good look at you."

Jamie huddled behind her, as if he, too, sensed something wasn't right.

"Please, sir, can it not wait until tomorrow? Jamie has stayed up far past his bedtime in order to be presented at the party."

The man shook his head and took a step toward her. "I'll not be here on the morrow. I've found what I came for."

Heather lifted her chin. "And what is that?"

The rogue grinned and ran his gaze down her body, making her feel dirty. Making her want to run and find Lucas.

"Your son doesn't resemble you in the least. How long have you been married to that blackguard brother of mine?

The insolent cad. "Mr. Reed and I aren't married. I'm Jamie's governess."

The man muttered something she couldn't make out and ran his hand over the dark stubble on his chin. "If only I'd had a comely wench like you for a governess, I might not have turned out to be a cut-throat pirate."

Heather placed her hand over her throat and swallowed

hard. "You're a pirate by choice."

The man leaped forward, grabbing the front of her dress. "You know nothing about me, missy. Because I had the misfortune to be born minutes after my brother"—he spat on the floor—"Lucas inherited all of our father's wealth while I got nothing."

Heather knew a man like this would take advantage of a weak woman, so her best hope was to face him head-on and not let him know her legs were trembling so hard she felt certain they'd give out any moment. "I'm sure Lucas would be happy to share with you if you were to cease your pirating and return home. Your mother misses you."

He snorted a scoffing laugh.

"Aunt Heather? I'm scared." Jamie clutched the back of her skirt.

"Ach, boy." The pirate glared at him. "Reed men aren't frightened of anything. Quit hiding behind those petticoats and prove you have a backbone."

Heather shoved the pirate, and he took a step back, grabbing her arm with one hand. "Jamie, quick, run to your father."

"Stand fast, boy!" A *chink* of steel on steel filled the room as Marcus Reed drew his sword.

"Nay! Jamie, run!"

Heather saw the man's fist only a second before it smashed into her head. She plunged into a realm of pain and darkness.

sixteen

Lucas charged into Heather's bedchamber, his heart nearly breaking in two when he found it empty. Pushing through the door into Jamie's connecting room, his frantic gaze took in the empty chamber. Lucas hurried to the piazza, searching in all directions. His hands raked through his hair, pulling it loose from its tie. He staggered back into the room and collapsed onto the bed.

"No! Please, God. No."

He couldn't lose Heather.

He couldn't lose his son.

"God, help me."

A moan sounded behind the open door to the piazza, and he bolted up, wishing he had a sword. His eyes landed on a pair of shapely ankles and Heather's gown. Relief washed over him like the warm sun after a turbulent storm. He knelt down beside her.

"Are you hurt, my love?"

Heather moaned and reached for her head. A stream of blood flowed from a swollen cut on her forehead and ran down her cheek. Her eyes suddenly widened, and she lurched to her feet and staggered through the room. She grabbed his arm, her distressed gaze searched his. "Jamie. Please tell me he didn't take Jamie."

A deep chasm opened up in Lucas's chest where his heart had been. He didn't have to reach the house to know that Jamie wasn't there. Nothing could hurt him more than loving his son—and Marcus knew that.

"Oh, Jamie." Heather's sobs filled the room. Lucas drew her against his chest and closed his eyes.

"You've got to go after him."

He thought of his oath to God never to sail again. How could he break such a devout promise to his heavenly Father?

Yet he could not allow his brother to get away with Jamie. The poor boy must be frightened out of his wits. Like a pendulum, Lucas's thoughts swung from one point to another and back. He had to go after Jamie. He couldn't break his word. He had to save his son.

Heather released him and stepped back, staring at him with an incredulous gaze. "Lucas, you've got to go—before they reach open seas. Each moment you waste in indecision allows them to get farther away. You've got to rescue Jamie."

"I can't. Don't you understand? I did things almost as vile as my brother, all in the name of my country. I promised God I'd never sail again."

Heather stared at him as if he'd turned green and lost all of his hair. "God would never hold you to such an oath. 'Tis all your own doing." She grabbed his arms and shook him, her brown eyes wide. "You've got to save your son."

A war raged within him. "If I fail to keep my promise to God, what kind of man would I be?"

Richard burst into the room holding Lucas's sword in the air like an avenging angel. When he saw Heather, his relief was evident.

She rushed to his side. "Please, sir, take me to the docks. We've got to rescue Jamie."

Richard's confused gaze dashed to Lucas and back. "Marcus has the boy?"

"Aye, and Lucas refuses to go after him because of his *precious* oath." She spat the words as if spewing a foul substance from her mouth.

"What does she mean?" Richard asked.

Lucas gazed up at the ceiling where the light from the wall sconces danced like sails in the wind. He rubbed the back of his neck, feeling ripped apart by his indecision. He'd changed from the carousing youth he'd been and given his heart to God, but now when he needed Him most, he felt betrayed. "God, how could you have let this happen again?"

" 'Twas not the hand of God that did this vile deed, but the evil of man," Richard said. "Don't be doubting your faith, Lucas, for you'll need it more than ever if you hope to track down your brother."

"But what about my pledge? I gave up sailing as penance because of all that I did before and during the Revolution."

Richard shook his head. "Lucas, you're my best friend, but that's just plain fanatical. God has forgiven you, and you don't need to punish yourself that way. God doesn't ask it of you. But He does expect a father to protect his children, and you've got a son who needs you. You're the only one who can save him. Just think how Marcus will warp his mind if you do nothing."

Lucas listened to his friend's earnest words and saw hope burn away the anger in Heather's eyes. He walked outside to the piazza railing and stared up at the ebony sky. Was it true? Had he needlessly punished himself all these years?

When he couldn't find Deborah, he'd given up on sailing. Perhaps he'd made that oath because he'd so miserably failed. His ship hadn't carried him to his beloved, so had he just walked away from it all and used God as a convenient excuse?

He heaved a heavy sigh. God was love. Forgiveness. He wouldn't take away something Lucas loved as punishment. If Lucas believed that, he was equating God with Marcus. And there was nothing in the least about God that was similar to his brother. He tightened his grip on the railing as he thought of Jamie. How dreadfully frightened the boy must be. He would expect his father to rescue him.

Hope rose in Lucas's heart like a ship on a swell. He pounded his hand against the wooden rail, knowing what he had to do. Straightening his body and his resolve, he spun around and marched into the room, taking his sword from Richard. He clapped his friend's shoulder. "Thank you for setting me straight. You're a good man."

"So, you're going after them?" his friend asked.

"Yes."

Heather sucked in a gasp, rushed forward, and fell against his chest. "Oh, praise be to God. Thank you, Lucas."

Heedless of Richard's presence, he held her tight with one arm, keeping the sword well away from her. He kissed her hard, showing her the depth of his love. When he pulled back, a grin tugged at his lips at her shocked expression. "Pray for me, beloved. Pray that I find them fast and return with our son."

"Aye, pray I will, but you're not going without me."

❧

Heather held tight to the gunwale as Lucas's ship glided across the open seas. The scent of salt tickled her nose, and the brisk wind pulled her hair loose from its bindings. High above her, sails snapped.

Once they'd set sail, Heather's heart sunk like a ship torn asunder at the magnitude of the task before them. How did one find a single vessel on such a vast sea, especially in the dark of night? Why, they could sail right past another ship and not even know it. She shivered as the cool breeze tugged at her clothing, damp from the sea spray.

"You should try to get some sleep." Lucas joined her at the railing.

She shook her head. "I can't. I'm too worried about Jamie.

I keep wondering if he's scared. Has he been mistreated? Is he locked away below ship in a dark hole?"

She turned to face Lucas, her heart aching with such a fathomless pain that she didn't know if she could survive it. "What if he hurts Jamie?"

Lucas brushed tendrils of loose hair from her face. "I don't think he will. He'll gain nothing by doing that."

"What did he hope to gain by taking him?"

Lucas stared out at the black sea. "At first, I thought he'd taken you."

" 'Tis my fault he took Jamie." Heather fidgeted with the edge of her cuff.

He took hold of her shoulders. "No. It is not."

Heather nodded, tears making her eyes gleam in the moonlight. "Aye, but it is. I told Jamie to run and get you while I tried to keep your brother away from him. Perhaps if I hadn't done that, he would have taken me instead of Jamie."

"Shh, enough of that."

Lucas pulled her into his arms and pressed her head against his chest. Her chill fled at the warmth of his body.

"My brother is a brigand. A scoundrel. He takes pleasure in hurting me, but I don't think he'd do damage to a child."

"But how will we ever find them?"

"Things are not as bad as they seem. There are only a handful of places a rogue like my brother can make port without the authorities coming for him."

Heather leaned back and gazed up at him. "But what about you? After fighting the British like you did, surely you must also be a wanted man."

He didn't answer for a while. "There's truth in what you say."

"If you are captured on the open seas, you'll be taken back to England. I've put you in danger by insisting you go after Jamie."

He ran his finger across her cheek, sending delicious chills down her spine. "I would have gone after him anyway. I was foolish to hesitate and think I was breaking my vow. I know more than most how big God's arms are and how much He forgives."

Even with God's help, Heather didn't see how it was possible to lose a child and ever get over it. She felt as if she'd die if they didn't find Jamie. Tears stung her eyes, and a sob slipped out as she fell back into Lucas's arm. "He's so little. So alone."

Lucas laid his cheek atop her head. "He's not alone. God is with him."

Her tears overcame her, and she wept against Lucas's chest. What if they never found him?

They stood together, Lucas with his feet braced apart to stand steady on the rising and dipping ship, and she in the shelter of his arms. She recalled how he'd called her *beloved* back at the Charleston house. Was that just a slip of the tongue during an emotional time?

After a while, he loosened his hold on her a fraction. "Heather, there's something I want to tell you."

She leaned back against the side of the ship and gazed up at him. She could barely make out one side of his face where the moon illuminated it, while the other side remained dark. Just like the two brothers. Twins, carried together in the womb, born on the same day, but one was kindhearted and honest, while the other was a blackguard with no heart at all.

Lucas heaved a deep breath and took hold of her hand. "It's hard to believe how much things can change in a few short weeks. A month ago, I didn't know you or Jamie. Then you both sailed into my lonely life and made my world whole again." He cupped his hand around her cheek. "I don't want you to leave. Ever."

Heather's heart flip-flopped, but she was afraid to hope that he cared for her as much as she did him.

"I love you, Heather. Can you find it in your heart to marry a brigand like me and put me out of my misery?"

Her cheeks lifted in a smile, and joy flooded her like a rogue wave in a squall. "Aye. I'd love nothing more."

He pulled her to him and lifted her up at the same time, and his lips collided with hers. His were warm, demanding but gentle, and all her fears and worries fled. After a few moments, he set her down but held her close. "I love you so much. I never expected to find love again."

That thought sobered her, stealing her delight. Who had he loved? Surely not Miss Dupont? He'd told Heather that he had no feelings for the woman. And if he had loved before, why had he never married?

Lucas pressed his hand against her head and held her close. "You should rest. It's a good thing you've agreed to marry me, because your reputation will have flown south after you set sail alone with just my crew and me."

He said the words in jest, but she couldn't help thinking of her cousin. Had Lucas promised her the world then taken her virginity and left her alone to raise their son?

Heather shook her head. Lucas may have been reckless in his youth, but he wasn't like that now. Where were all these doubts coming from? "I am tired. All the excitement of the party and the tragedy afterward has worn me out."

"Then I shall escort you to my cabin so you can retire." He took her arm and tugged gently, but she didn't release the railing.

"Why am I going to *your* cabin and not one of my own?"

Lucas waved his hand in the air. "This is a cargo vessel, not a passenger ship. My cabin is the only one suitable for a lady. There's a lock on the door you're free to use."

The recent joy of the night fled at the slight bite in his voice. Had she offended him?

"Come. You're safe here. There's nothing to fear from me or my crew."

She allowed him to lead her toward his cabin, hating her doubts. Just when she thought her life was about to change, she couldn't rid her mind of all that Deborah had suffered at the hands of the man they'd both fallen in love with.

I'm sorry, cousin, for loving the man who caused you so much pain. Am I making a dreadful mistake? Has he truly changed, or am I living an illusion?

seventeen

Hands behind his back, Lucas paced the deck of the *Victory*. A week had passed, and he still hadn't located his brother. *Think! Where could Marcus have gone?*

He knew his brother, and Marcus would want him to give chase. It was all a game to him. Take what Lucas loved, because that was the only way to truly hurt him. First, it had been the woman he'd planned on marrying, and now, Jamie.

Could Marcus have guessed that Jamie was his own son? Did he know that Deborah had borne him a child?

Lucas strode to the bow and stared out over the glistening blue sea as the schooner glided swiftly across the waters. The scents of salt, pitch, and oakum filled his nostrils, and he breathed deeply. Oh, how he'd missed sailing. What a fool he'd been to believe that God would expect him to forsake something he loved so much. Lifting his face, he stared up at the brilliant sky. "Forgive me, Lord, for believing a lie. Perhaps I was merely punishing myself, when You'd already freely given Your Son to die for me. Please, Lord, grant me favor. Show me where Jamie is."

His clothing fluttered in the stiff breeze, and behind him, sailors lifted their voices in a jolly time, but jolly was not a word that described his mood. With all but the topsails unfurled, they traveled at a quick speed. Yet they still hadn't caught up with Marcus. He pounded on the gunwale. "Where are you, brother?"

Thoughts of Jamie assaulted his mind, causing him to rest little at night. He ached to protect the boy. To hold him in his arms again. To laugh at something Jamie said.

In a matter of days, he'd lost his heart to his nephew.

His son.

And also to a pretty, brown-eyed wench who wore her heart on her sleeve. He'd asked her to marry him, yet he saw the doubts in her eyes. What put them there? Had he ever given her reason to question his sincerity? To fear him?

His grip tightened on the gunwale. Maybe he should tell her the whole truth even though Deborah had pleaded with him in her letter not to let anyone know that Jamie wasn't his son. But shouldn't Heather know?

He was surprised that Deborah had never told her cousin the truth about Jamie's father. Yet she'd done it to protect her son. The child of a pirate would have little chance to live a normal life. A decent life.

And what if Marcus ever learned he'd fathered a son? He would have done exactly what he did: He would have come and taken Jamie.

Lucas had to believe that the boy's kidnapping was a sudden impulse. How could Marcus possibly have learned about Jamie?

Lucas suddenly remembered the trollop in Charleston who'd thought he was Marcus. She'd seen him with Jamie and had commented about the boy. Had the woman relayed the encounter to Marcus, even after Lucas had paid for her silence?

Without a doubt, that was more than likely.

But the biggest question of all remained unanswered: Where was Marcus?

Lucas searched his mind again, thinking of all the places he'd traveled with his father as an older youth. They'd sailed the Caribbean, searching for ports where they could purchase tropical fruit and other goods to import to the colonies. It was during those days that his love for sailing blossomed.

Marcus had joined them only on two occasions. Their father had succumbed to Marcus's pleas to take him and Lucas on their journeys. His father hadn't wanted Marcus along, partly because he caused trouble but also because he wouldn't inherit any of the Reed holdings and hadn't needed to learn the shipping business as Lucas had.

He thought about the time when they visited Virgin Gorda, one of the larger of the Virgin Islands. Gigantic boulders littered the shores in an area known as the Baths. He and his brother had climbed the enormous stones said to be remnants of a volcanic eruption. Lucas smiled at the memory of chasing Marcus and hiding among the boulders. It was one of the fondest memories he had of his childhood.

Lucas rubbed his arm—the one he'd broken on that trip. He'd climbed upon the largest boulders, yelling that he was the king of the island. Marcus had taken that as a challenge, shinnied up the same boulder, and promptly shoved Lucas off. The next thing he remembered was being back on board his father's ship with a head injury and a broken arm. That trip was the last one their father allowed Marcus to go on.

A sudden gust of wind yanked Lucas from his memory. His gaze roved up the mast, to the sails, and back to the deck. Men faithfully tended their duties, needing little assistance from him.

His thoughts drifted back to Virgin Gorda. Marcus had boasted that he'd return to the island again, and Lucas felt certain he had. Maybe one day he could take Jamie to see the large stones. But first he had to find him.

A flame of a thought burned into his mind, flickered, and then exploded as if someone had set fire to a barrel of gunpowder. Of course. Virgin Gorda. That's where Marcus had gone.

He spun around. "Helmsman! Change course. Southeast by forty degrees."

Lucas crossed the deck, searching for his first mate. "Unfurl the topsails, Mr. Burton."

"Aye, aye, Captain. Unfurl the topsails!"

Sailors scurried up the ratlines like monkeys on a jungle vine. Lucas strode to the quarterdeck and stood with his face to the wind. For the first time in a week, he felt sure of his course.

❧

Heather tugged on the last of her petticoats then looked in the small oval mirror that hung on the wall next to a map of the Atlantic. The swelling had gone down, but an ugly bruise remained where that nasty pirate had hit her. Picking up her horn combs, she held one in her hand and shoved the other into her hair, hoping to keep the stiff winds from flinging it in all directions. She smoothed down her hair then lifted the other comb. The ship suddenly canted to the right, throwing her off balance. The comb slipped from her hand as she was thrown backward into a chair. She grasped for a hold, but her hand slipped, and she was tossed to the floor.

Her arm collided with the hard wood, and a sharp pain stabbed her elbow. She clutched it and groaned. "What in the world?"

She wrestled her skirts and managed to gain her footing again. After locating her lost comb, she pushed it in her hair, effectively pulling the wayward tresses out of her face. Glancing in the mirror again, she noticed her cheeks looked pale in the dim light, so she pinched them then spun around. Something was happening. She could sense it. A change was in the air.

She exited the cabin and climbed the stairs to the deck. Squinting against the bright sunlight, she held her hand over her eyes and searched for Lucas. In the week that had passed since their last kiss, he'd been concerned for her welfare, but he hadn't touched her other than to escort her around the deck. Had he seen the apprehension in her gaze?

How could she love a man and also doubt his sincerity?

Her gaze landed on Lucas's broad shoulders, and her heart leaped. He stood so tall, erect, with his feet spread to balance his stance. He pointed aloft and said something to a sailor standing nearby. The small man scurried up the network of braided ropes and climbed into the crow's nest. Heather laid a hand over her heart. Did these sailors have no fear?

Lucas turned, his gaze landing on her, and he smiled. He strode toward her, setting her pulse dancing with each step he took. She longed to toss her doubts overboard and fall into his arms, but she restrained herself.

"My dear lady, how do you fare this morning?" He smiled, but his lovely eyes held apprehension.

Again her heart frolicked like a child skipping through wildflowers, and she despised herself for causing him worry. A smile tugged at her lips. "I am well. Thank you. I felt the ship veer in a different direction. Am I correct?"

"Yes." He grinned, and this time his eyes sparkled. "I remembered a place my father took Marcus and me when we were only boys of twelve years. I feel certain that's where we'll find him and Jamie."

Heather grasped his arm. "Truly? I do hope you are correct. My hearts aches for him."

Lucas stepped closer, holding her hand in his. "We will find them. The good Lord is on our side, and I fully believe He reminded me of Virgin Gorda."

Heather's brows lifted. " 'Tis an odd name. What kind of place is this?"

Leading her around the deck, he explained about the island and its huge boulders.

"But what does Virgin Gorda mean?"

Lucas chuckled, drawing her gaze. She loved seeing him cast aside his worries.

"Legend says that the island was discovered by Christopher Columbus and that he named it Virgin Gorda because the land resembled a fat woman lying on her side."

"How peculiar."

"True, but the island is as they say. You will see when we arrive."

She swallowed hard. "Do you really think we'll find Jamie and your brother there?"

He nodded, his dark hair falling over his eyes. She longed to reach up and brush it back but, instead, clasped her hands in front of her. "I do. I've prayed all week and believe God brought that memory to mind so that I'd go there."

"I've prayed, too. More than I have about anything."

Lucas rested his hands lightly on her shoulders. "We will find them. I won't stop searching until I do."

"I don't know how to thank you. Jamie is like my own son."

He brushed the back of his fingers across her cheek, a longing gaze filling his eyes. "He *is* my son. I won't stop searching until I find him."

Heather smiled up at him. What would life be like as his wife?

She couldn't deny that she cared for him. Even loved him.

But would her doubts ruin any chance they might have for a happy marriage?

Lucas smiled and leaned down, kissing her forehead. "Let us see what we can find for you to eat. It's time you broke your fast."

One thing for certain, she would marry Lucas. After first losing Jamie back at Reed Springs and now being away from him this long, torturous week, she could not bear to be parted from him again.

eighteen

At sundown two days later, the *Victory* drifted into a cove. They carefully maneuvered around huge boulders that hid the bay from the sight of anyone sailing past the island. Closer to shore, yet a safe distance away, Lucas recognized his brother's ship floating on the still waters.

"Lower all sails, and tell the men to keep silent," Lucas told his first mate in a loud whisper. He stared at the lights of the campfire on the beach and knew Marcus and his men couldn't see them where they hid behind a wall of giant boulders. In the distance, he could hear the revelry of pirates as they drank their ale, played games of chance, and challenged one another to fights. With God's blessing, he hoped they could sneak ashore and steal Jamie back without anyone getting hurt.

"What is yer plan, Captain?" Mr. Burton asked.

"We'll wait until they are further into their ale and then attack them."

"Forgive me for questioning you, sir, but don't you think it would be better to locate the boy first? What if he's on their ship?"

Lucas rubbed his chin and considered his first mate's words. "You're right. If we attack the men on the beach and Jamie is still on the ship, someone might harm him when they hear the ruckus. Perhaps we should send a couple of men to scour the ship and see if Jamie is there first."

Mr. Burton nodded. "A grand idea, although it could take a while to search the whole ship."

"We have all night. Send Mr. White and Mr. Henning. They're our best swimmers and are less likely to be noticed than a rowboat. Be sure to instill in them the importance of keeping quiet. And bring me my spyglass."

"Aye, aye, Captain."

The man quietly strode off. Lucas focused on the dancing blaze across the bay. *Keep Jamie safe, Lord, until I can rescue him.*

Marcus wouldn't willingly let the boy go, but would he harm Jamie to keep Lucas from getting the child back?

His brother had harmed an innocent woman—done the worst thing imaginable—but had he gone so far off the deep end that he would hurt a child?

He'd told Heather no, but now he wasn't certain. Marcus wanted Lucas to pay for the way their father had treated him. And he *had* paid—he had suffered Deborah's loss. The pain from that horrific event still haunted his sleep on occasion. He should have searched longer for her. Should have found her and brought her home.

He had failed Deborah.

But he would not fail his son.

❧

Heather's knees ached from being bent in prayer on the hard floor for so long. Even her skirts no longer seemed to cushion them. She rose and walked over to the porthole and peered out. She could see nothing in the inky blackness, only her reflection staring back. Somehow it made her feel not so alone. The steady rolling of the ship had stopped, and she'd heard the splash of the anchor earlier. They had arrived at the islands, but she feared going outside. What if Marcus's ship wasn't there? What then?

A soft knock sounded on the door, and she rushed to answer it. Lucas's face appeared in the darkness as the light from her lantern illuminated it. His gaze darted past her to the light. He took her hand, led her to the bed, and lifted her onto it.

Heather laid a hand over her pounding heart. What was happening? She opened her mouth, but he held two fingers over her lips, then turned and extinguished both lanterns. The room plunged into deep darkness.

Lucas's footsteps crossed assuredly toward her. She scooted back farther onto the bed until her back hit the wall.

"All lights must remain out. We've arrived at the island, and a ship is here. We must stay dark and silent so my brother doesn't discover our arrival. I've sent some men to search his ship."

"How long will it take?"

"I don't know. Most of the ship's crew is on the beach from the sound of things, so I'm hoping that my men can handle any left on board."

"Do you think they will find Jamie?" She heard a rustling, and then his hand found hers, warming her and driving away her fears.

"If he's on board, my men will find him. If he isn't, we will sneak off ship and try to find him on the island."

Heather clenched his hand, knowing the danger he'd be in. She realized in that moment that she'd miss Lucas as much as Jamie if anything should happen to him. "I desperately want Jamie back, but I don't want you to get hurt."

He pulled her forward until she slid off the bed and stood in front of him. His hand found her cheek. "Shh, I will be fine. Don't worry."

"But you don't know how far your brother will go. What if he orders his men to kill you?"

He heaved a heavy sigh laced with the scent of coffee, warming her face. "I don't believe he will. Marcus is like a disobedient child who causes a ruckus but then wants to be loved afterward. I think he's in pain, and I long to help him. If he'll only let me."

Heather laid her hand on his chest. "Be careful. I saw the hatred in his eyes. He had no qualms about knocking me to the floor."

"God will be with us. Try to sleep and not worry."

"I cannot sleep, knowing all that could happen tonight."

"As you wish, but I must ask you to remain in your quarters. Darkness covers the ship, and you could get hurt if you wander about. Please stay in your bed. I will come to you as soon as I have news."

She clutched his shirt in her tight grasp. "Promise?"

"Yes," he whispered. "I promise."

He stood in the darkness, his hand to her face. His thumb caressed her cheekbone, and she longed to turn and kiss his palm. But such an action seemed too forward.

She'd had a full week with nothing to do but walk the deck, pray, and read the Bible in Lucas's chamber. She'd realized that she'd been letting her doubts rule her. Lucas had done naught to earn such misgivings. He captained his ship efficiently, and even when she'd seen a man mishandle a sail, causing it to tear and have to be repaired, Lucas gently reprimanded him and encouraged him to be more careful in the future. She was certain other captains would have severely punished the man for damaging something as vital to everyone's survival as a sail.

Lucas remained kind; he took time to visit with her and never once behaved in a dishonorable fashion, even when he walked her to the cabin door each evening. He'd never lied to her as far as she knew but took special efforts to keep her informed. She'd been foolish to let her doubts steal her future with Lucas. She'd never find another man as good as he.

His other hand touched her cheek. "I'm going to kiss you, my dear, unless you object."

With her heart thundering in her ears, she shook her head. His mouth found hers, and she received his kiss, letting him know that her heart belonged to him. Her hands slid up his chest, and she wrapped them around his neck. He teased her mouth with his, nipping her lower lip, then returning for a full kiss. After what seemed mere seconds, he pulled back then drew her to his chest, nearly crushing her in a fierce hug. His rapid heartbeat pounded in her ears. "Do you have any idea how much I love you?"

"Aye, I believe so."

"I'd love nothing more than to stand here and kiss you all night, but alas, that isn't the wise choice." His voice sounded husky, as breathless as she felt. He lifted her onto the bed again. "Stay here tonight, but lock the door after I leave. I can't keep my mind on finding Jamie if I have to worry about something happening to you."

"All right. I shall stay here and pray. But please let me know if you discover anything."

He kissed her cheek and stepped back. "I will."

Quickly, he crossed the room and exited, shutting the door behind him. Heather slid off the bed, felt her way across the cabin, and held out her hands, carefully searching for the door and then the lock. She finally found and secured it and made her way back to the bed.

The inky black of the room pressed in on her. Getting up on her knees, she reached for the porthole over the bed, wrestled with the latch, and finally got it to unlock and open. A warm breeze, salty with the scent of the sea, drifted in, bringing with it the sound of revelry. Men laughed, and raucous cheers sounded in the distance. She swallowed hard. What would happen to her if Marcus won the battle?

"Please, Lord, keep Lucas safe, and show him where Jamie is."

❧

Lucas paced the deck of the *Victory*, pausing every few minutes to lift his spyglass and search the dark water between the ships. He rechecked the position of the waxing crescent moon, a mere sliver of light. Several hours had passed, and yet he'd heard not a sound from the direction of his brother's ship. Either his men hadn't made the swim successfully or they'd boarded and secured the ship and were searching it even now.

"Help them find the boy, Lord," he muttered softly. Lifting the spyglass, he searched the shore near the campfire. The loud ruckus had softened, and he suspected that many of his brother's men were passed out in a drunken stupor by now. He could make out the reclining bodies of only a half-dozen men around the fire. Where were the others? Sleeping outside the circle of light?

A gentle splash sounded to his left. His hand flew to his cutlass, and he cautiously gazed over the side.

"H'lo the ship," a loud whisper pierced the silence.

"That you, Henning?"

"Aye, Captain."

"What of the boy?" Lucas tossed down a coil of rope, making sure one end was securely attached.

"We have him, sir."

"Thank the good Lord." Lucas glanced up at the ebony sky and nodded his gratitude toward the heavens.

"Grab hold of me neck, Jamie, lad. Keep silent like I told ye to, and don't let go." Mr. Henning prepared to climb up the side of the ship.

Excitement surged through Lucas as he peered down at the three silhouettes in the stolen rowboat—two large and one small. His son was being returned. He tapped his palms on the gunwale, wanting—needing—to hold Jamie in his arms again. "Hurry, man."

A grunt sounded below; then the rope jiggled and a scraping along the side of the ship grew nearer. Mr. Henning's head appeared over the side, a wide grin on his face. "We did it, Captain."

Jamie peeked up with wide eyes. "Papa?"

Lucas lifted the boy off his mate's shoulders, while two sailors hoisted Mr. Henning aboard ship. "Are you hurt, son?"

Jamie shook his head but his grip on Lucas's shoulders tightened. "Nay, but I was scared."

Lucas winced at the thought of the poor boy, alone and frightened. "Didn't you know that I'd come for you?"

"I prayed you would."

"That's a good boy. God showed me where to find you." He squeezed his son in a fierce hug, pleased that Jamie kept his voice low. Lucas's heart felt whole again. How was it possible to love Jamie so much in such a short time?

"That pirate looks just like you; did you know that?"

"Yes, he's my twin brother."

Jamie rubbed his eyes. "But he's mean. He's not nice like you are."

"Well, let's hope you don't have to see him again."

"Are we going home?" Jamie yawned. "Is Aunt Heather here?"

"She is, and she'll be wanting to see you." Lucas turned back to his men. "How many are aboard my brother's ship, Mr. Henning?"

"Only two, sir. Mr. White and I managed to conk them out. Then we tied them up and gagged them whilst we searched the ship. Found the boy and made haste to return to the *Victory*. What say ye now? Do we go ashore and battle the rest of them scallywags?"

Lucas stared at the shore. He wanted to deal with his brother, but part of him wanted to take Heather and Jamie and flee. If he did, would they ever be safe? Would the threat of Marcus returning and taking Jamie again always hang over their heads?

He had to deal with his brother. "Mr. White, take Jamie to Miss Hawthorne in my cabin and stand guard outside the door until I return."

"Aye, aye, Captain." He reached for Jamie, and the boy went, but he cast a longing gaze at Lucas.

Suddenly the sound of metal clanked against the wooden deck. Lucas turned toward the noise.

"Pirates!" a sailor yelled.

Lucas spun back to Mr. White. "Go! Guard them with your life."

The sailor nodded and hurried across the deck with Jamie in his arms. Lucas's sword made a *ching* as it slid from the scabbard. Pirates spilled over the starboard side of the *Victory* with war cries spewing from their mouths. His men were well-trained and fought back, man-to-man. Metal clanged against metal.

Lucas lifted his sword and fended off a pirate who looked unsteady on his feet. The man lurched sideways, took three quick steps, and fell overboard. Lucas could only hope the rest of his brother's men were as far into their cups as that fellow.

The roar of men filled the night air as Lucas searched for his brother. Mr. Henning had his hands full with a black-haired pirate. Lucas conked the rogue on the head with the pommel of his sword, and the man dropped to the deck. Mr. Henning nodded his thanks, wiped the sweat from his brow with his sleeve, then turned to engage another brigand.

A shout rang up, and the fighting slowed. Once again someone yelled to cease fighting, and slowly the pirates backed away from Lucas's men. His gaze finally located his brother, and his heart dropped to his feet.

"No! Do not harm the boy," he cried, crossing the deck in wide strides. Mr. White lay unmoving on the deck, his forehead bloody. The sight of Marcus with his knife at Jamie's throat chilled Lucas to the bone.

"Move! Get out of my way!" With a lantern in one hand, Heather squeezed between two sailors and gawked at the scene. Her eyes widened when they landed on Jamie. "Nay!"

Lucas motioned to Mr. Burton to keep Heather out of the way. The first mate took the lantern from her and handed it to another sailor then grabbed Heather around the waist with one thick arm. She pounded his forearm and kicked her feet in her effort to get free.

"Aunt Heather," Jamie wailed.

"Well, if this ain't a perfect picnic." Marcus sneered at Lucas. "You thought you could sneak in and take the boy back without me noticing?"

"Out of my way." Lucas pushed through the crowd as another lantern flamed to life. "Your quarrel is with me, brother. Don't hide behind the boy."

Marcus lifted his chin and glared back. "You'd like me to turn loose of him, wouldn't you?"

"Of course. I'll not lie. Set him free and fight me."

Marcus lifted the knife closer to Jamie's throat, and the boy whimpered. "Take another step closer, and I'll kill your son, brother."

nineteen

"Nay!" Heather screamed and fought the man who held her tight in his beefy grasp. Her heart pounded so hard she thought it would burst from her chest. She looked at Lucas, but his gaze was directed at his brother.

Two more lanterns were lit, illuminating the ragtag group in a spooky glow. It seemed as if all on deck held their breath. Heather didn't want to believe that Lucas's brother could harm Jamie. *Please, Lord. Spare him.*

"There's something you should know, Marcus." Lucas cast a glance at Heather, and her heart jolted at the intensity of his gaze. He turned back to his brother. "Jamie is *your* son, not mine."

Heather blinked, trying to comprehend what he'd said. How could that be possible? Deborah would never associate with a pirate.

Was Lucas simply lying to his brother to save Jamie? Or had he been deceiving *her* all this time?

Marcus's expression went white; then it hardened. "Ah, so you'd try to trick me, would you?"

"No." Lucas closed the distance until he was just a half dozen feet from Marcus. "Jamie is your son. Deborah is his mother."

The knife lowered, and Marcus turned Jamie around and stared into the boy's face.

"Think about it," Lucas reasoned. "Jamie is five. You last saw Deborah six years ago. If you look into your heart, you know I'm telling the truth."

Marcus ran his hand through Jamie's hair, a look of acceptance on his face. Suddenly, he pushed the boy to the side, drew his sword, and pointed it at Lucas. "You stole everything from me, even Deborah. I loved her as I've never loved another woman, but she never cared for me. It was you she cried for at night. And now you mean to have my son?

"Nay! I won't allow it." Marcus lunged forward.

Lucas swerved sideways, dodging his brother's thrust.

"Captain!"

Lucas turned, and one of his men tossed him a sword. He lifted the blade and prepared for the next assault. "I don't want to hurt you, Marcus. Things don't have to be like this. I never wanted them to be."

Marcus regained his balance and held out his sword, waving it in the air. "Aye, it does. You've ruined my life, and I mean to see an end to yours."

In two quick steps, Marcus attacked. Swords clanged, metal against metal.

"Please, let me go." Heather kicked her captor hard and pinched the forearm locked so tight around her waist that she could hardly breathe.

Mr. Burton grunted and carried her forward, as if to better see the fight. Heather franticly searched for Jamie, all the while praying for Lucas. Swords clanged, and cheers filled the air, but she couldn't see the two she loved most in this world. Marcus had held the lad a moment ago, but where was he now? The arm around her waist loosened, and Heather took full advantage and went limp. She slipped right through the man's arm and rolled away. She quickly untangled her skirts and stood. Mr. Burton, so engaged in his captain's battle, never noticed she'd gained her freedom.

Heather rushed behind the sailors, searching for Jamie. She pushed past a smelly man and looked everywhere.

"Aunt Heather!" Jamie squeezed out from between a barrel and the hull of the ship and stood.

She rushed forward and hoisted him in her arms, while sailors and pirates alike cheered on their captains. "Are you hurt?"

He shook his head and clutched her forearms tightly, tears swimming in his eyes. Heather carried him to the quarterdeck steps and helped him up. From her higher vantage point, she could see the two brothers—identical in features but so different in all other ways—battling for their lives. She cuddled Jamie and watched the melee as sword banged against sword. Brother fought brother.

What would happen to her and Jamie if Lucas didn't survive?

"Please, Father, give Lucas the victory."

Marcus stumbled backward and fell against the main mast. He stood as if dazed. Lucas waited, not attacking. She wanted to urge him on, to have him seize the opportunity, but she couldn't ask him to kill his own brother, even though she doubted Marcus would have any misgivings about doing so to Lucas.

Marcus stood and charged his twin with a loud roar. Lucas leapt backward, tripped on a pirate's outstretched foot, and fell to the deck.

The pirates cheered.

Heather gasped.

She wanted to turn her head, but the scene below held her captive. She held Jamie's face against her side, not wanting him to witness the heinous duel. "Save Lucas, Lord."

Sneering, Marcus sauntered forward, keeping his sword on his brother. "Methinks I'll enjoy living in that fine house of yours and raising my son in it. Tell me. Where *is* Deborah?"

Lucas wiped his sleeve across his bloody mouth. He tried

to rise, but a pirate's boot to his shoulder held him down. "Dead," he yelled. "She died far away from everyone she loved because she was too ashamed to return home after you were done with her. God forgive you for what you did."

A vile laugh filled the air, sending chills up Heather's spine. "Somebody help him," she screamed.

Marcus glanced up at her, grinning. "That wench of yours will do fine to replace Deborah in my bed and to raise the boy."

Lucas struggled again to rise. "She'll never be yours."

Marcus pointed his blade at Lucas's heart. "Aye, brother, she shall."

A movement below caught Heather's eye. Mr. White lurched to his feet, swiped the blood from his brow, then lifted his arm over his shoulder and swiftly drew it forward. A knife glimmered in the light as it flew toward the pirate. Marcus bellowed and clutched his chest. A unified gasp rang out from the crowd as he stumbled backward and fell to the deck. Lucas jumped up and hurried to his brother's side. He knelt beside Marcus and reached for the knife penetrating his brother's chest, then pulled his hands back without touching it.

Heather held her breath, afraid to believe they might yet be saved and at the same time sorry that Lucas had to witness his brother's suffering. All was quiet, as if each man held his breath.

"I forgive you for all you've done. Call out to God, Marcus. It's not too late for you to be saved."

The pirate chuckled then coughed. "I've no need for God in life or death. You win, brother."

"No. . .please, ask God to forgive your sins. Life doesn't end here. There's an eternity with God that remains if you'll only call on Him." Lucas grasped his brother's shoulders.

"Nay. I will not." Marcus's limp hand fell from his chest onto the deck.

Heather grieved for Lucas and the pain she knew he was enduring, but she couldn't help being relieved that his pirate brother was no longer a threat.

Lucas knelt with his hand against his forehead. She longed to go to him, to comfort him, but feared another fight might break out. She had to keep Jamie safe.

Grumbling arose from the crowd. A pirate shoved a sailor. Lucas shot to his feet. "There'll be no more fighting this day. My brother's men are free to return to the island."

"What of our ship?" a large man called out.

"Your ship will be torched, but you may live—as long as you throw down your swords. There's produce and wild game a'plenty on this island to feed you for a long while."

Heather watched Lucas's men as they kept their swords trained on the pirates. In spite of their grumbling, one by one Marcus's men dropped their weapons, clambered over the side of the ship, and disappeared. She blew out a deep breath as the last one jumped off the gunwale.

With the danger over, she felt as if she might collapse. She ruffled Jamie's hair. "We should get you to bed, lad."

"I want to see Papa—I'm hungry."

Smiling, she took his hand and led him toward the stairs. "Let's see if we can find you a bite to eat."

Lucas took the steps to the quarterdeck, two at a time, his relief evident when he saw them both safe. He took her in his arms, crushing her to him. Heather longed to hug him back, but she couldn't get over the fact that he'd lied to her. She pushed away from him. The light from the lantern below cast a flickering glow on the side of his face. Lucas gave her a quizzical stare.

"Is what you said true? Is Jamie your brother's son?"

Lucas glanced down at Jamie then picked him up. "Can this not wait?"

"Nay. Have you been lying to me all this time?"

Lucas closed his eyes and inhaled deeply. He strode to the stairway. "Mr. Henning, come up here."

The tall, lanky man hurried to do the captain's bidding. "Aye, sir."

"Take Jamie to my cabin."

The boy locked his arms around Lucas's neck. "Nay, I want to stay with you."

Lucas patted the lad's back. "Did I not hear you say you were hungry?"

"Aye." Jamie nodded.

"Then go with Mr. Henning. He will find you a bite to eat, and Heather and I will be down shortly."

Jamie glanced back and forth between them. "Promise?"

"Most certainly." Lucas nodded. "I will be down to tuck you into bed, just like I do when we're at home."

"All right." Jamie allowed Lucas to pass him to the sailor, and Heather watched them descend the stairs, not yet ready to see him go.

Lucas remained silent until they heard the door below close. "It was Deborah's wish that no one know. That's what she wrote in her letter."

Anger blazed through Heather at her cousin's betrayal. She had tended Deborah, cared for Jamie, and even risked her own life and Jamie's to bring him to Charleston. No wonder Lucas hadn't accepted the boy at first glance. He wasn't Jamie's father, after all. She pounded her fist against Lucas's chest, releasing her fear, anger, and hurt. "Don't you think I had a right to know the truth?"

"If Deborah had wanted you to know, she would have told you. She was only trying to protect her son." Lucas grabbed her wrists and held them.

"And what was I doing? I've raised him as my own all these years. Scrimped and saved to bring him here to you, when you're not even his true father."

"You think that matters to me? Did I not take him in as my own even though I faced ridicule and my family name was threatened by the gossip of an illegitimate son?"

Heather jerked away, turned her back to him, and strode to the side of the ship. She couldn't explain why she felt as if she'd been betrayed. Wouldn't she have cared for Jamie even if she'd known the truth?

She shivered, thinking what her cousin must have gone through in the hands of that pirate. Had he taken her by force? Or had she succumbed to his wiles and given herself freely?

Either way, Jamie was the son of a vile pirate. No wonder Deborah wanted everyone to think that Lucas was the father. But had she considered what it would cost him?

She heard his footsteps drawing closer and stiffened. He laid his hands on her shoulders. "You have a right to be angry. But I was only honoring Deborah's wishes. At the time, I didn't know that you'd be here long term or that I'd fall in love with you. Try to understand, Heather."

She hung her head, ashamed at her outburst. All he was doing was protecting Deborah and her son. Tonight's tension and Lucas's near death had paralyzed her, and then to learn the truth in such a horrible way. . .

She'd lashed out at him because of her fear. "I'm sorry."

He turned her around but just stood there, not touching her. "I never wanted to hurt you. I only told Marcus the truth to save Jamie. I was afraid he'd kill him just to get back at me."

"I feared the same. I do believe he meant to." Heather shook her head. "How could two brothers be so different?"

Lucas took hold of her hands. "I don't blame Marcus. Our father's favoritism drove a wedge of anger and bitterness in my brother and warped his mind. Nothing I did helped. I only made things worse by trying to be the peacemaker."

Heather squeezed his hand. "It's not your fault. Marcus made his own decisions. There are many younger sons of wealthy men who've made something good of their lives. Marcus could have done the same, but he chose not to." She wanted to tell him that she was sorry for his brother's death, but she couldn't voice the words, knowing they weren't completely true. She *was* sorry though that Lucas was grieving and that she'd vented her anger toward him. Stepping forward, she wrapped her arms around his waist and laid her head on his chest.

His arms encircled her. "If only he had repented. . ."

"Shh. . .you did all that you could."

Footsteps sounded behind them, but Lucas didn't release her. A man cleared his throat. "We await your orders, Captain."

"Send three men over to my brother's ship. Have them set free the men they tied up and let them swim ashore; then set the vessel afire."

"But what of the bounty aboard, sir? Mr. Henning mentioned a wealth of treasure was stowed below."

Lucas let go of her and turned to face his first mate. "I want nothing to do with stolen wares, Mr. Burton. Prepare to set sail at first light. And see to it that the men keep watch in case my brother's men decide to try and retake the ship."

"Aye, aye, Captain." Mr. Burton cast an odd glance at Lucas, and Heather wondered if he expected to get keelhauled for allowing her to escape. Then he spun on his heel and strode away.

Lucas wrapped his arm around Heather's shoulders, and

they stood facing the island. The sliver of moon prepared to sink below the horizon. A warm breeze tugged at Heather's hair and teased her skirts. After all that had happened tonight, she was almost afraid to feel. To hope for a future with Lucas.

"I need to spend some time in prayer. I wanted to run my sword through my own brother when he talked about making you his."

She felt him shudder. "Cease your worries. He can harm us no more."

Lucas lifted a hand to her cheek then ran his thumb over her lip, sending delicious chills racing through her. "You're skin is so soft. I love your brown eyes." His hand brushed over her hair. "And your hair is so lovely. You've a kind, generous heart. There's nothing about you I don't love."

Tears stung her eyes to think she had been ready to walk away from their relationship a few minutes ago. When she'd first brought Jamie to Charleston, she'd never expected to fall in love. She lifted her hand to Lucas's bristly jaw. "I feel the same way. I can hardly wait to awaken each morning, just to see your sky blue eyes, to listen to your voice. I'm sorry for getting upset."

Lucas chuckled. "I've no doubt that there will be many other times that I shall upset you, but with love and God's help, we can just as quickly set aside our differences and make up."

"Aye," she whispered.

He lowered his face until she felt his breath mingle with hers. "I believe my heart mutinied the day I first laid eyes on you. I mean to make you my wife, Heather Hawthorne. Have you any qualms almost that?"

She smiled and shook her head. "Nay. None at all."

His lips met hers, and Heather knew she'd discovered where she was meant to be. She never dreamed she'd find happiness in the land that had warred against her homeland and ultimately caused her father to give up on living.

But God moved in mysterious ways, and He'd certainly worked a miracle for her.

A Letter To Our Readers

Dear Reader:
In order that we might better contribute to your reading enjoyment, we would appreciate your taking a few minutes to respond to the following questions. We welcome your comments and read each form and letter we receive. When completed, please return to the following:

Fiction Editor
Heartsong Presents
PO Box 719
Uhrichsville, Ohio 44683

1. Did you enjoy reading *Mutiny of the Heart* by Vickie McDonough?
   ❑ Very much! I would like to see more books by this author!
   ❑ Moderately. I would have enjoyed it more if
   ____
   ____
   ____

2. Are you a member of **Heartsong Presents**? ❑ Yes ❑ No
   If no, where did you purchase this book? ______________
   ____

3. How would you rate, on a scale from 1 (poor) to 5 (superior), the cover design? ______________

4. On a scale from 1 (poor) to 10 (superior), please rate the following elements.

____ Heroine	____ Plot
____ Hero	____ Inspirational theme
____ Setting	____ Secondary characters

5. These characters were special because? ____________________

____

____

6. How has this book inspired your life? ____________________

____

____

7. What settings would you like to see covered in future **Heartsong Presents** books? ____________________

____

____

8. What are some inspirational themes you would like to see treated in future books? ____________________

____

____

9. Would you be interested in reading other **Heartsong Presents** titles? ❑ Yes ❑ No

10. Please check your age range:

❑ Under 18 ❑ 18-24
❑ 25-34 ❑ 35-45
❑ 46-55 ❑ Over 55

Name ____
Occupation ____
Address ____
City, State, Zip _____________________________________
E-mail ____